Charlie the Dog in...

Oodles
of
Poodles

ANDREW WOODING

Phoenix

Front cover and cartoons by Mike Kazybrid

British Library Cataloguing in Publication Data

Wooding, Andrew
Oodles of poodles.
I. Title
823'.914 [J]

ISBN 0-86065-815-5

Phoenix is an imprint of Kingsway Publications Ltd
1 St Anne's Road, Eastbourne, E Sussex BN21 3UN
Typeset by Nuprint Ltd, Harpenden, Herts
Printed in England by Clays Ltd, St Ives plc

To Derek, Lee and Lianne Smith,
for frequently opening up their home to me
and for going out of their way
to be friends.
Star Trek lives!

Author's Note

Some of the more observant readers among you may notice slight similarities between my 'Wow' Screen and the chronoscope in C. S. Lewis' *The Dark Tower*.

I hereby wish to make it clear that any such similarities are purely the result of my unoriginal mind.

Important Bit

The following is the amazing but true story of how Charlie Digestives met God, and how he came to be known as Charlie the Dog, a poodle detective in a world of human beings.

In order for the story to be fully understood, it is necessary to begin with a few short chapters about a pimply British schoolboy and his very first crush.

The schoolboy's name is Dickie Dustbin, and he isn't in a very good mood....

Part One

Dickie Dustbin's Superpower

1

It was a miserable Friday morning in Walbridge, England—dull and drizzly, and altogether rather unpleasant for those sorts of people who don't like dull and drizzly mornings. Dickie Dustbin was one of those people and he consequently felt miserable himself. However, it wasn't just the poor weather that was making him feel down.

There was a lot on Dickie's mind this morning as he walked to Heathlands Secondary School. It was tough being a thirteen-year-old teenager. Especially if you were a teenager in love. And especially if you were in love with a sixteen-year-old fifth-former who was going steady with Jonathan Matthews, the brightest and most athletic (and also most hand-some) boy in the school. Every time Dickie thought about Jonathan he wanted to throw up.

'Why is it that she goes out with that boring idiot?' he thought, frustratedly kicking an empty Coca-Cola can in the general direction of the school. 'He's nowhere near as interesting as I am.'

Jonathan, as a matter of fact, was not the boring idiot that Dickie claimed him to be. In fact, he was an exceptionally kind and warm-hearted individual, who was well liked throughout the school.

The object of Dickie's affections was Penny Green, another warm individual who, because of her reliability in the school over the years, had been assigned the responsibility of assistant school librarian. Dickie would often talk to Penny in the library whenever he felt lonely, and he loved the way she laughed at all of his jokes, even the ones that weren't all that funny. He also felt a great tingling sensation down his back whenever he told her about his problems and she smiled compassionately back at him. When Dickie first met her he had respected Penny for the considerate human being she was, but now that respect had turned into a deep love and it was driving him crazy.

There was a school disco that night. It was the Friday before the last week of term and, as on all Fridays before the last week of term, all the pupils would congregate at half-past seven in the school gym in various forms of attire, ready to dance the night away (or at least the next three hours) to the latest chart sounds, amplified almost beyond recognition. It was the thought of this disco that was especially troubling Dickie this morning.

'How on earth will I get her to dance with me?' he thought. 'The only thing I can think of is to impress Penny so much at school today that she'll have no choice but to dump that creep Jonathan and spend the whole evening with me.'

Easier said than done. What could Dickie possibly do to draw Penny away from Jonathan? Because Jonathan was such an outstanding pupil, there seemed nothing Dickie could do to better him.

'Hey, just a minute!' Dickie said, his thoughts

suddenly interrupted. 'Isn't that Coca-Cola can glow-ing?'

His muddled love life faded into the background, at least for the time being, while he bent down to retrieve the battered can. Sure enough it *was* glow-ing, and the more he stared down at it the more his amazement grew.

'Wow! This is really freaky! But the can's a bit grubby. I'll rub it so that I can see more of the glow.'

Dickie enthusiastically rubbed and rubbed with his shirt sleeve until most of the dirt had been trans-ferred from the can to his shirt, and then....

Kafoomph!

'Cough, cough! I don't think I'll ever get used to all this awful smoke!'

The voice belonged to an extraordinary thin gentleman with greying hair and a bushy moustache, who was wearing a pristine pin-stripe suit and a smart black bowler hat. One of the things that made him extraordinary was the fact that he was floating cross-legged above the can, coughing and spluttering and waving away as much of the smoke caused by his appearance as possible. Another one of his extra-ordinary attributes was his invisibility to everyone except Dickie, although Dickie did not yet know this.

'Wh-who are you?' Dickie asked when he had finally plucked up enough courage to speak.

'Who am *I*?' The man seemed rather offended. 'What a silly question! Why, I'm...erm...hang on a moment! Just who *am* I?'

After a few seconds of scratching his head, hoping that in some way this might reactivate some rusting memory cells in his brain, he said: 'I'm the genie of the Coca-Cola can! Yes, that's who I am!'

'Really?' said Dickie, now more excited than before.

'Yes, that's right,' said the man. 'I...' He stopped because he wasn't a very good liar. His conscience hurt him too much. 'Actually, no I'm not,' he eventually admitted, rather sheepishly. 'I'm really a criminal from the planet Yumslurp many millions of light years from here. I've been exiled to this can for a hundred earth centuries, and I'm only to emerge from it when people rub the outside.'

'Gosh!' Dickie looked delighted. The man's face, however, reflected the opposite end of the emotional spectrum.

'It's not so thrilling,' he said, with tears welling up in his eyes. 'How would *you* fancy being trapped inside a miserable aluminium container for ten thousand years? It's going to be sheer torture. Complete isolation, and all because I succumbed to a quick moment of temptation on Yumslurp with those 3,000 sticks of rhubarb and the custard. It's all wet and sticky down in that can as well. Yuck! They could at least have cleaned it out before transporting me there.'

After a few minutes of careful thought, Dickie bravely asked: 'Erm, even though you're not a real genie, will you be able to grant me a wish?'

'Unfortunately yes,' said the man. 'That's one of the requirements of my sentence here on this planet. Judge Cucumber on Yumslurp decreed that every time an earthling rubs my can, I will have to leave it for a few short seconds to grant the person his heart's desire.'

'Wow! Magic!' said Dickie.

'Not really,' said the man. 'Just highly advanced molecular reconstruction. The trouble is, I've never done this sort of thing before, so forgive me if I make a mistake. Now, what's your wish?'

'Gosh. That's a tough one.'

An excited Dickie leaned back against a nearby brick wall, thousands of exciting ideas buzzing all at once through his brain. But he didn't want to pick just any old idea. This was probably the only time in his life he was going to be granted this sort of wish, and he wanted to make the most of it.

'Now, let me see,' he said, thinking very carefully. 'I've always wanted the complete set of *Spider-Man* comics. Maybe I could ask for that.' Not much later he dismissed this idea on the grounds that he could always buy the set when he became a rich and famous film star. He needed to wish for something that he couldn't buy even if he had all the money in the world.

And then Dickie suddenly had a brainwave.

'I know,' he said. 'Why don't I ask for a super-power like Spider-Man's? I've always wanted to be a superhero.'

The pin-striped exile of the Coca-Cola can, who had been listening to Dickie all this time, took a small calculator-type device from underneath his bowler hat and said: 'Your wish is my meringue...or command...or however that phrase is supposed to go.' He said a few unearthly words while pressing a large red button on the device, then cheerfully waved goodbye. 'Farewell, my friend. Through the miracle of modern electronics your wish has now been granted. Use your superpower wisely and...well, thanks for being so understanding about this being my first time. Bye!'

Kafoomph!

When the second cloud of smoke had cleared,

Dickie was horrified to see that the 'genie' had disappeared. You see, it was all very well Dickie now having a superpower, but...well, he hadn't had a chance to ask that chap what his superpower actually was. The can had disappeared as well, and Dickie couldn't see it anywhere. He was understandably dismayed about the whole thing.

That dismay, however, soon turned into intense delight as an interesting thought suddenly occurred to him.

'Hey, wow!' he said, a bright cheerful smile on his face. 'I could use the superpower to impress Penny at school today. It shouldn't take me long to figure out what the superpower is because there aren't really that many, and Penny will be so bowled over by my new ability that she'll immediately fall in love with me and spend the whole three hours of the disco in my arms!'

Dickie Dustbin felt invigorated, and there was a fresh determination in his steps as he made his way towards the school. Love seemed to do that to him. He either felt downcast and depressed at his lack of progress in getting closer to Penny, or absolutely elated any time he seemed to have made a minor breakthrough in their relationship.

Now he was about to make a *major* breakthrough—joy of joys—and all he had to do was find out what his superpower was.

'Yippee!' he shouted joyfully, leaping high in the air and dropping most of the conkers and week-old Liquorice Allsorts out of his pockets.

And that was all he had to do....

2

It hadn't been a very good day for Dickie. Despite many different attempts at school to establish the identity of his superpower, he had not succeeded in any of them. He felt humiliated, and he looked very depressed indeed.

'It would have been okay,' he reflected, 'if it hadn't been for the fact that Penny was there every time I made a fool of myself. There's no way she'll want to dance with me now...and I still don't know what my superpower is.'

As you can see, Dickie was beginning to regret that he'd been granted his wish.

Dickie's first downfall (literally) had been outside the gates of Heathlands Secondary School. He had been boasting to a group of friends that he could fly (after all, that was almost bound to be his superpower since it was the most common one), and one of them had dared him to prove it by jumping from the gate.

'Okay, I will,' he had said to his disbelieving comrades. 'Give me a leg up and I'll show you.'

The subsequent heroic dive from the top post was up to Olympic standards. The same, however, could not be said of the landing.

'Oh no!' screamed Dickie in mid-air when he realised that he wasn't flying—and that he was about to collide painfully with the ground.

Dickie panicked and, with arms and legs waving madly in all directions, he loudly bounced along a thin strip of grass in front of the school and eventually came to rest at the feet of Penny and Jonathan, standing hand-in-hand.

'Dickie! Whatever are you playing at?' said an extremely concerned Penny. Penny knew Dickie to be a thoughtful and also very quiet individual, and his dramatic leap to her feet seemed rather out of character.

'Oh...er...nothing,' he said shamefacedly, staring nervously up at her nostrils. 'Just trying something out, that's all.'

Penny smiled, and offered him a hand up.

'Well, just don't hurt yourself, okay?' she said.

'Okay,' agreed Dickie, and he gratefully clasped her hand as she pulled him to his feet.

'Wow!' thought Dickie afterwards, smiling contentedly to himself as he wiped the grime from his school uniform. 'She *must* be in love with me. She wanted to hold my hand!'

Then Dickie's spirits sank as he looked up and saw Penny and Jonathan walking away, giggling and innocently kissing each other on the cheeks. He thought perhaps they might be giggling at him and he shuddered at the possibility. Then he heard his mates at the gate laughing as well, and he summoned up as much strength as he could to look unhurt as he hobbled back to join them.

He cursed his stupidity in assuming so soon what his superpower was and hoped that this embarrassing incident would soon be forgotten. (Although Dickie enjoyed making fun of other people, he found it very hard to take similar mocking remarks when they were directed towards him.)

And so it had been throughout the day.

At breaktime he had decided to see if he could walk through solid matter, and he promptly smashed into a nearby pane of glass. (Penny, coincidentally, had been walking in the school hall on the other side of the pane at the time of impact.) The glass didn't shatter, but Dickie's delicate nose had not been so fortunate and it wouldn't stop bleeding for ages.

At lunchtime he had decided to test for invisibility by walking into the school staff room and willing himself to disappear. Needless to say it hadn't worked, and needless to say Penny was there with the main school librarian when he was told off for intruding on private territory.

On the way home from school he figured that his superpower might possibly be running very fast, and he broke into a super-quick sprint which abruptly ended when he tripped over a stone. His exercise books flew everywhere, many of them landing on an alarmed Penny's head who just happened to be in front of Dickie when he fell.

'Oh no,' he thought on the ground, blushing and trying to think up a convincing excuse for his apparent strange behaviour. 'Yet again I've embarrassed myself in front of my potential future wife.'

And now Dickie was retracing his steps to Heathlands School, not particularly looking forward to the school disco due to start in half-an-hour's time.

Absent-mindedly kicking an empty Coca-Cola can in the general direction of the school, he angrily mumbled to himself about nothing in particular...then stopped suddenly in the street, a stunned expression on his face.

'Crikey!' he said, staring incredulously down at the ground. 'I don't believe it! Lightning *does* strike twice!' The 'lightning' he was referring to was the glowing Coca-Cola can three feet in front of him. It was clearly the same can he had encountered this morning, and with it, Dickie assumed, there must also be the same 'genie' that had given him his superpower.

Excitedly he picked it up, and he rubbed frantically with his shirt sleeve until....

Kafoomph!

'Cough, cough! Not again! Who is it *this* time?'

The man was floating cross-legged in the air again, and he was wearing a long white nightgown and a thin dangling hat with a fluffy woollen ball hanging from the end. He was yawning, and he looked very tired.

'It's me...Dickie Dustbin,' said guess who. 'I was the person you granted a wish to this morning.'

'What?' The man looked (and also sounded) very shocked. He rubbed his watery eyes, then peeked down at the current owner of the can through the gaps between his fingers. 'But it can't be! Every time I activate the molecular reconstruction device and return to the can, I'm supposed to be automatically transported to another part of the world. The idea is that nobody gets a wish from me more than once. After all, fair's fair you know.'

'Well, obviously it didn't work,' interjected Dickie.

'Yes, obviously,' the man concurred. 'I guess I'll have to tinker around with the transport mechanism so that this area isn't graced by my presence again...or at least not for a very long time. Look, I'm sorry. That means I can't grant you another wish.'

For a moment, Dickie looked despondently down at the ground. He had had many disappointments today already, and this latest one did little to cheer him up.

Then he looked up and timidly asked the man: 'Erm, listen...I don't suppose you could just...er...somehow check and tell me what super-power you gave me this morning? You don't know how hard it's been trying to figure it out for myself.'

There was no reaction from the man. His eyes were open, and he looked as if he was in a trance.

'Please?' Dickie added hopefully.

Still no reaction.

'Pretty please?'

Then the man suddenly jolted as if he had woken up with a start.

'Gosh. Sorry about that,' he apologised. 'I was just thinking, it'll be ten thousand years before I can have Yumslurp custard again. Sigh. I'll really miss my custard. It'll be the longest ten thousand years I'll ever have experienced.'

For a brief moment tears started welling up inside the man's eyes, but then he bravely fought this embarrassing display of emotion and said: 'Anyway, what was it you wanted me to do for you?'

Dickie quickly repeated his request, and the man kindly complied by taking that small calculator-type device from underneath his hat and pressing a small recall button on the side.

'What?' was Dickie's horrified reaction when the answer had been given to him. 'Do you call that a superpower? That's not going to help me very much! Poo!'

The man couldn't see the reason for Dickie's bitter reaction.

'What do you mean?' he said. 'People on Yumslurp would love that sort of superpower. After all, we eat an awful lot of food up there. Especially custard.'

And then he started to weep hysterically, his des-pondent head shaking in his trembling hands.

'No more custard for ten thousand years!' he wailed. 'Just the thought of it—sob—is too much for me to handle! Snort!' (The snort was him blowing his nose on his nightgown.)

'I'm sorry! Weep!' he continued, pressing a large red button on his device and feebly waving goodbye. 'I don't like crying in front of people, so I'll have to leave now. Ta-ra, and—sob—have fun with your superpower.'

Kafoomph!

'Wait! Cough. Stay here!' Dickie demanded, spluttering because of the smoke. 'I want a new superpower. I....'

But his demand came too late. The man and his can had disappeared, and Dickie was left feeling more depressed than before.

'Blaah! What a pathetic superpower!' he cursed. 'How can I impress Penny with that?'

Two of Dickie's friends—John Adams and Guy Davidson—walked by just then, one of them trying but not succeeding to restrain a laugh, and the other looking very puzzled.

John, the puzzled one, said: 'Hello, Dickie. What was all that noise for just then? We saw you shouting back there, but didn't see anyone you could be shouting at.'

'If you ask me,' said Guy, giggling while he spoke, 'I think Dustbin's gone a bit potty. You saw the way he kept chasing after Penny Green today. I reckon he's in love.'

Dickie didn't say a word. He merely hung his head in shame, too embarrassed to look up at his friends.

John and Guy exchanged concerned glances, and John patted Dickie on the back.

'Come on, friend. Cheer up,' he smiled. 'Let's walk to the disco together. It's going to be great tonight.'

This was followed by a few more encouraging pats on the back and an artificial smile from Guy, but they did nothing to lift Dickie's deep gloom.

'Yes,' he thought sarcastically in response to this last statement. 'It'll be a bundle of laughs.'

He didn't say a word as he followed his schoolmates to the school. He hoped that Guy didn't *really* believe he was in love. Romantic involvement was much too soppy for his image, and yet it was true. And it didn't seem as if he would be able to express that love of his tonight.

If only he could think of a way to make Penny fall in love with him.

If only she would take him in her arms tonight and carry him away to some remote desert isle where they could dream for ever together, never to be disturbed by the shattering concrete intrusions of twentieth-century reality.

If only....

'Sigh.'

3

Not in the mood for dancing, Dickie Dustbin sat on the steps outside the main school building for the first few minutes of the disco, watching all his mates arriving either on foot, on bicycles, or in their parents'

23

cars. To his delighted surprise Penny arrived alone on her bike, and not following Jonathan on his bicycle as he had expected.

'Hello, Penny,' he greeted her cheerfully. 'Where's Jonathan tonight?'

'Oh, he's working,' Penny answered, chaining up her bicycle by the entrance. 'Don't you remember? He has a part-time job at Wimpy's.'

'Wow!' thought Dickie, smiling on the inside, but trying on the outside to look very sympathetic towards Penny's misfortune. 'Maybe tonight won't be so bad after all. With no Jonathan about Penny'll be desperate to dance with someone, and she's bound to turn to me first!'

'But I don't mind all that much,' Penny continued. 'I wouldn't have been able to dance with him anyway. I've been asked to serve at the tuck shop all evening.'

I won't tell you what word came to Dickie's mind next, but it was sort of the opposite of 'Wow!' and it definitely wasn't very nice. Still, Dickie seemed to handle Penny's confession rather well. He smiled and said, 'That's very kind of you to give up your time like that,' and waved goodbye to her as she walked into the school building. But inside he was hurting very deeply, and it made him wonder why love could sometimes be so cruel.

'Rats!' he then thought, sitting sombrely back down on the steps. 'This is even worse than before. Even if I'd had a proper superpower she wouldn't have been able to dance with me...and it's all because of that stupid tuck shop!'

For most of the rest of the disco Dickie sat at the back of the tuck shop room, alternating between looking down at the ground and feeling sorry for himself and looking up at Penny handing various customers chocolate bars, crisp packets, or soft drink tins (or combinations of all of these, depending upon the wealth of the customer). Every time Penny served someone of a masculine persuasion, Dickie felt insanely jealous.

How like a goddess she seemed then—a radiant Olympian beauty. Her peaceful smile touched Dickie profoundly, with waves of warm excitement rippling through his entire body. Her graceful movements sent Dickie's heartbeat way past its normal level, and his toenails curled upwards as every single particle of his being reacted to the love that he felt inside.

Oh, how he wanted her. Oh, how he wanted to be with her, to get married to her and to live in her joyful presence for the rest of his life. Oh, how desperately he wanted to dance with her tonight. And yet he knew he couldn't. And he felt lonely and rejected and depressed.

He also needed to go to the toilet. He stood up, walked quietly out of the room, and wasn't seen for the next ten minutes. Maybe he spent those minutes crying, but there was no way of knowing. No one could see into the confines of his silent, private cubicle.

Mr Ryfield, the deputy headmaster of the school, walked over to Penny at that moment and whispered a suggestion in her ear.

'You must be kidding!' she soon replied, but she smiled while she spoke and she secretly thought his idea was fantastic.

'No, I'm not,' said Mr Ryfield, also smiling. 'As well as boosting our sales, it'll be a lot of fun. Will you do it?'

'Yes, of course,' smirked Penny, and then Mr

Ryfield walked away, waving goodbye and mentally preparing his announcement for the school gymnasium, which was doubling tonight as a dance floor.

Ten minutes later Dickie emerged from the school toilets, looking very mean and kicking every inch of available wall space in sight, or at least everything below four feet.

He had taken all the sadness he could for one day, and now he was angry. He was expressing the deep rejection he felt in the form of open rebellion. But the rebellion didn't last for long.

'Stupid disco!' he shouted. 'I should never have come. It's been nothing but...gaah! My foot!'

The tears started welling up inside his eyes again, this time for physical rather than emotional reasons.

After sitting down in the corridor for two minutes, gently massaging his throbbing toes, a subdued Dickie heroically limped back to the tuck shop room, expecting to resume his sulking fit for the last half-hour of the disco. The scene that greeted his eyes when he entered the room, however, meant his sulking fit was soon forgotten.

The room was full of chattering excited boys (and a lot of not-quite-so-excited girls) queuing up at the tuck shop while laughing, singing and generally being extremely raucous. Dickie wondered what all the commotion was about, and he walked up to John Adams at the end of the queue, who he hoped would reveal all.

'Hello, John!' he said, trying his best to sound cheerful. 'What's going on?'

'Oh, haven't you heard?' said John. 'There's going to be a competition.'

'Really? What is it?'

'Whichever boy eats the most Mars bars in one go can have the last dance with Penny Green tonight.'

'What?'

'That's right. And the *girl* that eats the most gets to dance with Mr Ryfield...only no one has seemed too interested in taking up his offer so far. Poor chap. The last I saw of him he was running to the staff room, crying. What do you think, Dickie?... Dickie?...Are you all right, Dickie?'

Dickie didn't say a thing, but his face said everything. His incredulous but smiling mouth was open as far as his jaws would allow it to open; his astonished eyes, though fixed on John, seemed to be gazing at something three million miles away; and his excited ears, not normally prone to waggling, were flying backwards and forwards at faster-than-light speeds, fanning the air as they went. Dickie was overjoyed.

After ten seconds of this, Dickie then leapt high in the air, reaching up with his outstretched arms and letting out a blood-curdling: 'Yeeeeeeahoooooooo!'

There was then complete silence, and Dickie was suddenly brought back down to earth again.

'Oo-er!'

Every eye in the room, including Penny's, was now staring at poor Dickie Dustbin, nervously shaking at the back of the queue while turning a deep shade of red.

'Oops!' he thought, each stare in the room penetrating deep into his self-consciousness. 'I've gone and made an idiot of myself again, haven't I?' Momentarily he wished that his superpower was teleportation because he wanted to get out of this embarrassing situation as soon as possible, but then he remembered what his superpower actually was and a joyful smile returned to his lips.

'Sorry! Got a bit carried away there,' he informed the crowd, feeling that some sort of explanation was necessary. Then he pulled a wallet from his pocket to see how much money he had. 'Hmm. 60p,' he said, carefully counting the cash. 'That won't be enough.'

Sensing that the excitement was over, the people returned to their laughing and singing and extreme raucousness. John, however, wanted to pursue the matter further.

'So what was all that about then, eh?' he asked, annoyed that he wasn't in on the reason for Dickie's excitement. 'Why the sudden outburst?'

John was obviously desperate for this information, and Dickie craftily used this as the basis for some bargaining.

'Have you got any money on you?' he asked.

'Yeah. About six quid,' said John. 'Why do you want to know?'

'Good. A fiver ought to be enough,' Dickie reckoned. 'Lend it to me and I'll tell you all about it.'

At first John was reluctant to hand over the money, but soon his curiosity outdid his reluctance. He loaned Dickie the five pounds on the strict condition that it would have to be returned on a certain date in the not-too-distant future (eg, tomorrow morning, so that he could buy most of this week's comics).

Then he repeated his question: 'Why do you suddenly seem so happy?'

When Dickie had whispered the answer in John's ear John started to laugh, partly through disbelief but mainly at the thought of what Dickie was about to do.

'Twenty Mars bars? All in one go?' he sniggered.
'It can't be done.'

'Can't it?' smiled Dickie, confidently clutching the
money in his hands. 'You just wait and see!'

4

Five minutes later, twenty-three eager boys were
sitting round a large table in the tuck shop room,
possessively holding their Mars bar supplies close to
themselves. All were looking smugly across the table
at each other because all were optimistic about their
chances of dancing with Penny tonight.

Most of the boys up and down the table had about
three or four Mars bars each (with the maximum
being six), but right at the very end of the table was
Dickie with his tall mound of twenty. Those nearest
to him were making fun of him because of this, and
they were whispering extremely negative and also
very rude comments to each other, most of them loud
enough for Dickie to hear. But Dickie was not
deterred by any of these. He was certain of the eventual outcome of the competition, and he was looking
forward to these people having to swallow their
derogatory remarks when he became the victor.

'Yippee!' he thought, ecstatic about his remarkably good fortune. 'I'll be dancing with Penny after
all, and I owe everything to that man in the Coca-
Cola can. I was really disappointed when he told me

that eating as much food as I like without gaining weight or feeling sick is my superpower...but it's all turned out so perfectly!'

Then Dickie looked admiringly at Penny Green, standing with a whistle in her hand at the back of the room with the other girls. Most of them looked pretty bored, except for good old Penny who was smiling enthusiastically and who looked as beautiful as ever. Dickie knew that in just a few minutes she would definitely be his, and the thrill that he felt at that thought was just...well, indescribable.

Dickie sighed as he basked in the pure joy of it all. 'What an exciting evening this is turning out to be.'

Not much later the whistle was blown by Penny to signal the start of the competition, and then the boys were off. All talking suddenly ceased, and the only sounds that filled the room, apart from disco music leaking in from the gymnasium, were twenty-three boys either noisily rustling Mars bar wrappers as they mercilessly tore them open, or greedily chomping away at the chocolate, impolitely slobbering and slurping as they hurriedly gobbled the food. It seemed like a race to the death, and at the moment everyone was running neck and neck...except for Dickie.

Dickie was calmly sitting at his place on the table, slowly unwrapping his Mars bars and placing them in a neat pile in front of him. Even though he was losing, he had a very smug expression on his face. No one else noticed, though—they were too engrossed in their own piles of chocolate, which were getting smaller by the second.

It was about three minutes into the competition that people started collapsing. One by one, nauseous green faces fell with deafening thuds onto the table, and some of the more energetic competitors fled the room in a mad dash for the toilet. And this was after only three or four Mars bars!

Five minutes into the competition there were only three competitors left: Guy Davidson who was on his fifth Mars bar, Robert Michaels who'd eaten four, and Dickie Dustbin, of course, who still hadn't eaten a thing.

And then twenty seconds later, Guy and Robert simultaneously collapsed backwards, their chairs crashing to the floor with quite a few spectators' toes being crushed in the process. They had both taken more than they could handle, and now only Dickie remained, tearing the wrapper from the last of his bars.

When he had finished, he looked up at everyone and enthusiastically announced: 'Okay, guys! Here goes!' And then the miracle happened.

In front of the crowd of astonished adolescents (Penny included), Dickie proceeded to devour his pile at the rate of one bar every three seconds. It was like a highly efficient machine. As soon as one Mars bar entered his mouth, his free hand would reach for another for him to digest. And so the pile shrank and shrank, until exactly sixty seconds later...success!

'Burp!' went Dickie, sitting back in his chair and contentedly patting his bulging stomach. 'Have I won?'

Every conscious mouth in the room let out an audible gasp, and there were more mad dashes for the toilet, even by people who hadn't eaten anything that evening. Penny couldn't believe what she had just seen, a feeling shared by most of her suitors. Yet none could deny what had just transpired, and soon their disbelief turned into wild admiration.

Loud applause filled the air, and Dickie the super-star stood up to take a bow.

'Thank you! Thank you, everyone!' he said, beaming from ear to ear and enjoying all the attention he was getting. He winked at John Adams, smiling back at him from his seat at the table. John had given up after two Mars bars, and although he felt sick he was pleased at his friend's success. He was also astonished that everything Dickie had told him about the man in the Coca-Cola can appeared to be true.

Penny walked over to Dickie after the applause had died down, and raised his hand high in the air to signify his triumph.

'The winner!' she announced. 'This handsome young gentleman has earned himself the honour of sharing the last dance with me.'

Then the applause increased again and Dickie sat back down in his chair, unable to take all this joy standing up.

And so he remained for the next several minutes, as the pupils slowly filtered out of the room and as Penny meticulously cleaned up the mess, some of it not so nice. But Dickie didn't notice any of this activity. He was smiling sweetly into the furthest reaches of outer space, dreaming of his dance with Penny and loudly cracking his knuckles, a sign of true bliss.

5

Penny soon took Dickie by the hand and said, 'Come on, dreamer. I'm taking you to the gym for your prize.'

Dickie seemed startled.

'What? Huh? Oh...er...yes.'

And then it suddenly dawned on him that it was finally going to happen. Everything he had hoped for these last few desperate months was now about to take place.

This was no dream now, no wishful thinking. This was reality—and reality has this disconcerting way of rudely barging in on your fantasies. Dickie was nervous, and for a moment he wished he could have just stuck to his fantasies. Nevertheless, he bravely gritted his teeth and followed Penny Green out of the tuck shop room.

More applause greeted the 'happy' couple as they entered the school gymnasium, hand in trembling hand.

'Oh no,' thought Dickie, pretending to be happy but feeling terribly self-conscious. 'Everyone's going to be staring at us. This should be a private thing. What if I make a mistake?'

The crowd urged Penny and Dickie forward to the front of the dance floor, and Penny followed their prompting while Dickie reluctantly tagged along.

The DJ gently faded out the record that was playing and made an announcement over the loud-speakers.

'Lay-deeth and gentlemen,' he started (the disc

jockey was the thirty-year-old school caretaker who had a lisp), 'will you pleeth give a warm hand for the winner of the Marth bar eating competithun, Mithter Dickie Duthtbin!'

Dickie didn't let on to the crowd that he felt awkward (and, more importantly, he didn't let on to Penny). He smiled and waved at them as they cheered back, but secretly he felt like being back in his bedroom at home, lying awake on his comfortable bed and dreaming about other things he could do.

'And now,' the DJ continued, sweating because he was nervous (he didn't like appearing in public too often), 'we will have the final danth thith evening. Hug your partner tightly, all you grooverth, and get ready for the latht thmooch of the night. Thmooch? Gathp! Thith ith too mucth for me!'

There was a hollow thump as the shy caretaker fell to the stage floor in an overload of excitement, and then the music started.

'Come on,' said Penny to a rather introverted Dickie. 'You're supposed to put your arms around me. Haven't you ever done this before?'

'N-no,' admitted Dickie, quivering at the lips.

Penny took pity on her suddenly reluctant partner and grabbed him by the wrists.

'I'm surprised,' she said. 'I thought you were more experienced than that. Still, there's a first time for everything.'

Penny pulled Dickie's arms up by her shoulders, and Dickie instinctively joined his hands behind her neck. It was awkward for him at first because Penny was much taller, but she made it easier by gently embracing him and pulling him closer to her.

Physical contact! Dickie was not used to it, and for

a second or two he felt what seemed like a massive electric charge racing through his entire body. Then he rested his head on Penny's jumper, enjoying the warmth of the pure woollen fabric.

'Hmm, this is good,' he said, letting go of all his tension and relaxing in Penny's arms.

'I suppose so,' said Penny, 'except I think we've forgotten something.'

'What's that?'

'Hugging each other is fine, but we really need to move around a little before it can safely be classified as dancing.'

'Oh yes. Sorry.'

The dance began well, and Dickie actually started to enjoy himself. He loved Penny deeply—the person he could talk to in the school library whenever he had any problems—and he almost found himself crying over how beautiful this whole experience was. He began to wonder why he had been worrying so much beforehand.

Not long into the dance, however, Dickie found all sorts of negative thoughts creeping into his brain: 'She's only doing this because of the competition. She would have danced with someone else if you hadn't won. She doesn't mean what she's doing. Why are you getting so emotional?

'She doesn't love you. You're too young and pimply, and Jonathan is much more attractive. Why should she give up Jonathan for you?

'How can you possibly have a romance with her? You're smaller than she is and nowhere near as clever. You couldn't keep a conversation going with her for longer than two minutes. Why don't you give up? It's a hopeless cause.'

Dickie tried not to think these thoughts, but he

found it very hard to stop. Soon the thoughts started to sink in, and Dickie began to build up a dislike for Penny. Why was she using him in this way? Why was she luring him into a false sense of love which she knew would not be fulfilled? Why was she treating him like a child and not as an equal; dancing with him out of pity and not because of love?

Before he knew it the dance had finished. The hall lights came on and people started walking away to the cloakroom. Penny gave Dickie a quick kiss on the cheek then headed towards the door.

'Wait! Where are you going?' Dickie asked, stroking his cheek and blushing slightly because he wasn't used to being kissed.

'The tuck shop room,' answered Penny. 'I need to tidy up in there and count the day's takings before I can leave for home.'

'But...is that it?' Dickie sounded bitter. 'Is that all there is between us? A quick three-minute dance and a kiss, and then back to the normal routine? It's as if nothing ever happened!'

Penny was taken aback by Dickie's reaction.

'What do you want from me, Dickie?' she asked. 'What can I do for you to make you feel better? Why are you talking this way?'

Dickie froze. He knew what the answer was. He was in love with Penny, and he wanted some definite assurance that she loved him back.

But he did not tell her this. He was too afraid of the rejection he would feel if she gave him a negative reply.

Penny persisted with her questions.

'Come on, Dickie. There's something wrong, isn't there? What is it? I want to help.'

'I....' Dickie started to speak, but found that he

couldn't continue. It was too hard for him to express what he was feeling. He turned away from her, but Penny stepped over to touch his shoulder.

'Tell me, Dickie, please. I won't be offended, honest. And I do want what's best for you.'

'I...' Dickie continued, but he never finished his sentence. Instead, he requested: 'Could you...erm... could I have another kiss, please?'

At first Penny didn't know whether to laugh or cry. It dawned on her that the poor kid must be in love with her. Wisely she didn't laugh because Dickie was looking very earnest. This guy was serious.

Penny looked sympathetically down at him. She realised that this matter needed to be sorted out tonight, and she gently took him by the hand.

'Come on,' she said. 'I think we should get to the privacy of the tuck shop room. It's time you and I did some serious talking.'

Dickie refused to budge.

'I know what you're going to say,' he grunted. 'You're going to tell me how beautiful your relationship with Jonathan is, and that one day I'll have the same sort of relationship myself when the right girl for me comes along.'

Penny looked thoughtfully down at the ground.

'Dickie, I have a confession to make,' she announced. 'I...I'm not in love with Jonathan.'

'What?'

'That's right.'

'But....'

Penny hesitated for a bit, wondering how much more she should tell Dickie. Eventually she blurted it all out. Dickie needed to know where she was coming from.

'Do you believe in parallel universes, Dickie? Universes that are similar to *our* universe, only with very slight changes?'

'I suppose so. I don't know.'

'Well, there's a universe called the poodle universe that has a poodle planet earth. And this earth is just like *our* earth except that the main life-form is poodles instead of human beings. Poodles that stand upright and wear the same sorts of clothes that humans wear. Poodles that eat cornflakes in the mornings and that commute to poodle cities. Poodles that compose symphonies, and poodles that go to church. Poodles that....'

'Hold it! Hold it!' interrupted poor Dickie, trying to take all this in. 'Why are you telling me this? What's this got to do with us...or with Jonathan?'

Penny took Dickie by the hand again.

'Come on,' she said. 'Follow me to the tuck shop room. I'm going to tell you a story involving a very famous detective and his loony professor friend. I think you might be interested.'

Part Two

The 'Wow' Screen

6

This is the story that Penny told Dickie:

It was a weekday morning like any other weekday morning in Walbridge on the poodle planet earth. Poodles were rising all over town, either to go to work, to school, or to get their husbands and pesky kids off to work and school so that they could get back to sleep again.

Lovely Selina Scottydog, as gorgeous as ever, was reading the news on BBC1's *Breakfast Time*.

'...down his wellington boots,' concluded Selina, and she went on to the next news item.

'Professor Alfred Boggles, possibly the cleverest man in the world next to Frank Bough, will be unveiling his latest invention at the museum in his home town of Walbridge this morning. Dubbed "The 'Wow' Screen", the professor claims it has the ability to display clearly what is happening in other universes. The professor is with us in the studio right now. Erm, Professor...'

'Yes, dat iss beink my title, yes.'

'...why have you called your new invention "The 'Wow' Screen"?'

'Becoss ven you look into der screen you vill almost certainly be sayink to yourself "Wow!" Ha ha.

Dat iss beink my little joke here.'

'Thank you, Professor,' said Selina. 'And now an interview with Charlie Digestives, the world-famous detective, about his triumphant capture yesterday of the evil Pickled Onion Monster.'

'Aaweaouwgh!' yawned Charlie Digestives as he fiercely stretched his poodle arms and mouth at the same time. This may seem like an extraordinarily rude thing to do on breakfast television—especially on *BBC* breakfast television—but, you see, he wasn't actually *on* the television. He was in his bedroom in Walbridge, and he had just been woken up by his alarm clock at exactly the same time as his pre-recorded interview was on the air.

'Aaweaouwgh!' he yawned again, sitting up in bed, and as he did so he experienced something so mind-bogglingly extraordinary that it caught him completely off his guard. For the briefest of moments Charlie felt something like a mighty wind blasting through his brain, clearing away all the cobwebs that were in there and helping him see life as it really was. It was exhilarating. All his fears and worries disappeared, and he felt for once that his life had meaning—that he was an important part of some wonderful plan. Somehow he knew, in that instant, that despite all the wars and the suffering in the world, someone very powerful loved this planet and was making sure that everything turned out all right in the end.

One blink and the feeling was gone, and his fears and worries returned. It had only lasted a fraction of a second, but it so shook Charlie that he had to sit silently on his bed for a while to think through what it meant.

He was brought back down to earth again by an

elderly voice downstairs singing a Kylie Minogue song totally out of tune. He remembered then where he was, and he promptly shrugged his shoulders, putting the experience down to sitting up so suddenly while still half-asleep. Dismissing it as unimportant, he calmly put on his dressing gown and slippers and marched downstairs.

When he entered the living room he saw himself with Selina Scottydog on the colour Sony Trinitron. He quickly turned this off (he found it embarrassing watching himself on television), and he quietly sat down at the dining table at the back of the room. His maid, Ethel, was working in the kitchen, still merrily slaughtering the Kylie Minogue song. It was chronic.

'Good morning, Ethel,' Charlie shouted to her. 'What was for breakfast this morning?'

'Er...um...two boiled eggs and a hot buttered piece of toast,' Ethel shouted, embarrassed because she hadn't realised that anyone had been listening to her 'singing'.

'But the eggs exploded and the toast burned, right?' guessed Charlie.

'That's right, sir, as usual,' confirmed Ethel, and she entered the living room with a bowl of unidentifiable goo in her paws. (She was wearing an attractive pink dress, Doc Marten boots and a Mexican sombrero.) 'So you'll have to make do with my home-made porridge again.'

'Oh.' Charlie sounded very unenthusiastic, and it wasn't hard to guess why. He didn't like porridge, and he especially didn't like Ethel's home-made porridge (which tasted remarkably like stewed socks in vinegar—with three spoonfuls of soggy semolina thrown in for good measure).

'Somehow I don't feel hungry any more,' he

informed her, wishing his groaning stomach would stay quiet during his feeble attempt at amateur dramatics. 'I think I'll skip breakfast this morning.'

'Oh, okay.'

Ethel wasn't the most efficient maid in the world, but she was cheap and that's why Charlie employed her. She was eccentric to say the least, and she was probably well into her nineties, though no one knew her exact age. Some unkind people had suggested that the best way to find out her age would be to chop her in two and count the rings on the inside. But Charlie would *never* do a thing like this.

As Ethel sadly took the porridge bowl back to the kitchen, Charlie went to inspect the two items of post that had obediently been left next to his armchair: a large parcel that had obviously been wrapped in a hurry, and a bulging padded envelope.

Charlie reached for the parcel first because it was closer to his greedily grasping paws, and he proceeded to tear off the outer layer of wrapping paper. When he had done this he found that he was left with a slightly smaller parcel, wrapped with different coloured wrapping paper.

'That's odd,' said Charlie. 'Why does this parcel have two layers of wrapping when one would have done?' Little did he realise that further surprises were in store.

Ethel, hearing her boss muttering to himself, raced from the kitchen and urged at the top of her voice: 'Save the string. It might come in handy later!' She then ran back into the kitchen to search for her string box in which she kept unwanted bits of string and other pieces of scrap which might someday, given an infinite amount of time, come in surprisingly useful.

While she did this, Charlie unwrapped the parcel

again and found another, smaller parcel resting on his lap.

'Oh look,' observed Ethel as she raced back into the living room, dropping a cotton reel or two onto the floor. 'It has lots of Father Christmases on the wrapping paper this time.'

'Do you know what this means?' said Charlie in a sudden burst of light humour (and, indeed, the humour was very light).

'No, sir,' said Ethel, ignorant as usual. 'What *does* it mean?'

'It means,' said Charlie with a smile on his face, 'that whoever sent this parcel must be from the North Pole!'

'Ooh!' shrieked Ethel, not realising that this was a joke since it was up (or down) to Charlie's usual standard (ie, it was feeble). 'You're better than Cliff Richard any day!'

'Thank you,' said Charlie, accepting his maid's admiration, though he wasn't quite sure what this admiration was for. Then he held another unwrapping session, and, to his surprise, he found a weather-beaten, century-old, Sainsbury's reject cardboard box.

'Well, it's about time we had a change from wrapping paper,' Charlie commented, unable to think of anything better to say, but feeling that he ought to make an observation anyway.

'You'd better keep that as well,' put in Ethel. 'As I always say, you never know when you might need a cardboard box.'

Charlie took a smaller cardboard box from that cardboard box, and out of that cardboard box he found a smaller cardboard box with an even smaller cardboard box inside it. He thought this would go on for ever, but luckily he soon found that he was wrong. After a few more cardboard boxes, he reached a green folder which contained a large brown envelope.

'I bet there's another envelope inside that one,' guessed Charlie, and he was right.

'I don't want the envelopes,' sniffed Ethel, waving them away. 'You can throw them away if you want to.'

'Thank you for your kind permission,' responded Charlie, knowing that Ethel would not realise he was being sarcastic.

After a few more envelopes, Charlie found a small white paper bag.

'I wonder what's in there?' he said.

'Probably another paper bag,' suggested Ethel.

'I hope not.' Charlie dipped his hand inside and took out a half-eaten Mars bar with fungus growing on the outside.

'Golly! What was *that* doing in there?' he said as he examined the false teeth marks on the chocolate. 'It looks revolting!'

All of a sudden Ethel started to laugh, a thing she had not done—at least not in public—for sixty-nine years.

'What's so funny?' asked Charlie, surprised at his maid's sudden outburst and annoyed that for once he was not in on the joke.

'Well,' explained Ethel, 'do you remember when you were going to have a birthday party a few years ago, but no one turned up?'

'Yes, I do,' said Charlie. 'The party coincided with the first showing of *Star Wars* on British television.' He nodded his head, but he still felt left in the dark.

'But I fail to see what this Mars bar has to do with my unsuccessful birthday party.'

'Don't you remember?' said Ethel. 'That parcel you just opened was what we were going to use for the pass-the-parcel game.'

Ethel resumed her uncontrollable laughing fit, obviously making up for lost years, but somehow a smile failed to reach Charlie's lips. A world-famous detective needs all the time he can get to concentrate on his many important duties, and this had just been an unpleasant waste of ten minutes.

'Wa-haa-haa!' shrieked Ethel, rolling about on the dusty carpet, her sombrero and loose poodle wig sliding from her head. 'I...hee hee...must have left the parcel there when I was tidying up the storage room this morning!'

Charlie was definitely not amused.

'Give me strength,' he murmured, looking heavenwards. Then he leaned forward to reach for the remaining item of post.

Carefully avoiding the first-class postage stamp (Ethel was still saving those for a ten-year-old *Blue Peter* fund-raising appeal), Charlie tore open the top of the padded envelope and pulled out the large green publication that was inside.

'Oh goody,' he went as he peeked at the bold heading on the glossy front cover. 'It's the latest mail-order catalogue from Harrods.' Ignoring his maid who was still chortling merrily on the floor, he tried to find the 'Toys' section.

'I hope they've got those rib-ticklingly funny clockwork false teeth that chomp up and down and always cause a stir at parties,' he wished out loud, and he licked his lips with wild anticipation.

But before he could locate the right pages, a special wafer-thin tape recorder fell from the lower end of the catalogue. Charlie groaned as he bent down to pick it up, knowing all too well what it was. The catalogue was just a clever way of hiding this top-secret recording.

Charlie routinely pressed a small red button on the front which said 'Press', and the ultra micro-tape inside instantly started playing.

'Hello, Charlie,' said the voice on the tape. 'This is Agent W from the ACME Peace Corporation speaking. If you can't hear what I'm saying, please turn the dial which says "Volume".'

Charlie couldn't hear anything, so he nimbly twisted the dial which said 'Volume'.

'The weather is fine here,' continued the voice on the tape. 'There are a few clouds in the sky, but we can still see the sun through the window and it is quite warm. Is Ethel okay? I'm okay. Are you okay?'

'Ah, that's better,' said Charlie. 'I can hear him now. That sounds like Agent W from the ACME Peace Corporation.'

Ethel immediately stopped laughing, and a look of extreme uninterest appeared on her well-lined face.

'Oh, it's the ACME Peace Corporation,' she grunted. 'I'm not interested in your affairs with them. I think I'll go back to the kitchen and do the washing up.'

Charlie did not stop her from leaving the room, and he sat well back in his armchair to hear what Agent W had to say. (W was one of Charlie's closest friends, and he was the only other person in the ACME Peace Corporation who liked yoghurt sandwiches with HP Sauce.)

'As you've probably guessed, we have another

case for you to work on,' W Explained. 'The infamous Clothes Line Snatcher has been sighted again, and he is now in your area, up to his usual tricks.'

'Oh no!' screamed Charlie, standing upright on the armchair while biting his pawnails. Then he sat back down again, embarrassed at his over-reaction.

'We think he may try to raid your garden,' warned W. 'It's been announced by him in the past as being one of his big ambitions, so you'd better be prepared. We need to get this highly dangerous criminal in jail where he belongs, before he causes too much damage in the gardens of innocent Walbridge-itians...or onians, or onions...or whatever they're called.'

'I'll do my best,' promised Charlie.

'Great,' said W, who had guessed what Charlie's reaction would be. 'And now it's time for me to sign off in the usual way.'

Charlie stood up and saluted as a crackly recording of 'God Save the Queen' played over the cassette recorder's small loudspeaker while Agent W sang along to it. (He was singing out of tune, but he wasn't doing it deliberately because this would have been very disrespectful towards the wonderful Royal Family.) When it had finished, a gruff, elderly voice appeared on the tape.

'Hello, this is X speaking,' revealed X (Charlie's boss, and the head of the ACME Peace Corporation). 'I have one more thing to say before the end of this recording.'

'I wonder what *that* could be,' thought Charlie.

X continued. 'This tape will self-destruct in ten seconds!'

'Oh no!' Charlie had heard this sentence many times since he first started working for the ACME

Peace Corporation, yet it always seemed to catch him off guard. Unfortunately for the often-replaced living room window, this morning was to be no exception.

Charlie quickly grabbed the micro-player and threw it in the general direction of the newly-repaired back window. He then leaped behind the tower of cardboard boxes that Ethel had left on the floor, hoping that this would be adequate shielding from the explosion.

The cassette player smashed through the glass and landed in Ethel's well-kept compost heap in the back garden, now filled to the top with steaming, freshly-cooked porridge.

'Oops,' went Charlie, seeing where his throw had landed it and imagining the future consequences of this.

Ten seconds after X's announcement there was an almighty bang, and fragments of smelly compost—some of it as old as Ethel herself—showered the building.

'Erm, Ethel,' said Charlie, re-emerging from behind the cardboard boxes and looking very embarrassed indeed.

'Yes?' said Ethel, returning from the kitchen at Charlie's command.

'Remind me to tell the gardener to clean up that mess in the garden the next time he comes round.'

'Yes, sir,' noted Ethel. 'Very good, sir.'

Charlie sat back down in his armchair, a thoughtful expression on his face. He had to figure out a way to capture the Clothes Line Snatcher, a dangerous foe who must be stopped as soon as possible before hundreds of housewives throughout Walbridge had nothing to hang their washing on.

How anyone could stoop so low as to steal innocent people's clothes lines Charlie just could not understand. No one would have even considered doing something like that ten years ago. He was living in evil times indeed.

7

Professor Alfred Boggles looked worriedly down at his wristwatch as he drove back to Walbridge.

'Gulp!' he said. 'Dere's not enuff time!'

It had been a good morning for him so far, being interviewed by the lovely Selina Scottydog on BBC breakfast television. But now it was getting late. His demonstration at the Walbridge Museum was at 10 am, and it didn't look as if he would get there in time to set up the 'Wow' Screen.

The poodle Penny Green was pretending to read a newspaper while eating her cornflakes at the breakfast table, but she was really thinking about the school trip to Walbridge Museum this morning to see the 'Wow' Screen. It seemed so incredible—a screen that actually showed what was happening in parallel universes almost exactly the same as hers but with minor differences.

Jonathan Matthews was quickly finishing off a history essay at the desk in his bedroom. It was hard for him to concentrate because he was too excited at seeing the 'Wow' Screen later in the morning at the Walbridge Museum.

Charlie Digestives was busy in his back garden, making odd, almost inhuman (inpoodle) noises. Ethel wondered what the noises were, and she peered at him through the kitchen window.

'What are you doing?' she asked.

Charlie angrily looked up from his work, obviously not too pleased at this disturbance.

'I'm taking down one of the posts that holds up our clothes line!' he bellowed. 'What do you think I'm doing?'

'Oh?' said Ethel, still not exactly sure what Charlie was up to. 'What's that for?'

'It's just a little idea I have to help me catch the dreaded Clothes Line Snatcher,' he answered. He was pleased that he now had someone to explain his idea proudly to, and he regretted the fact that he had been so rude to her. 'If you come out here,' he invited, 'I'll show you how it will work.'

Charlie was no longer in his dressing gown. Instead he was wearing jeans and a 'Battersea Humans' Home' tee-shirt. He normally wore a suit and tie, but since he wasn't meeting any ACME Peace Corporation clients today he figured he could get away with wearing these casual clothes. Ethel didn't have on her sombrero any more because she'd realised how ridiculous it looked. Now she was wearing an Indian head-dress.

'So how *is* it going to work?' Ethel asked Charlie when she had joined him outside.

Charlie didn't answer this immediately. Instead he put on one of his best smiles which usually signalled bad news for Ethel, and said, 'I'll need your help.'

Ethel groaned. She knew what Charlie's maid-participation schemes were normally like. She sighed, then reluctantly gave in, saying, 'All right then. What do I have to do?'

Charlie's smile widened. 'Stand there,' he ordered, pointing to a beetle-infested hole where the post used to be.

Ethel did as she was told, but she obviously wasn't too happy about it. 'What has this got to do with your plan?' she demanded. She did not like standing on soily spots where clothes line posts used to be, and there were more important things she needed to be doing, like tidying up the house.

'Well,' started Charlie, 'the Clothes Line Snatcher is going to raid our back garden some time today. After all, the ACME Peace Corporation told me, so it must be true, right?'

'I suppose so,' agreed Ethel. 'But why have you got me standing here?'

'I'll explain it to you all in good time,' promised Charlie. 'Just bear with me while I see whether you are suitable for the part of a substitute clothes line post.'

'Substitute clothes line post?'

'First put your paws by your side,' commanded Charlie.

Ethel did this obediently.

'Now put the other end of this clothes line in your mouth.'

Ethel sighed, wondering what the point of this exercise was. She took the end of the clothes line to please her boss, and placed it in her mouth, biting down hard with her dentures.

'Perfect,' said Charlie, admiring for the first time his maid's thin figure. 'Absolutely perfect! You know, this brilliant plan of mine might just work!'

'*What* might work?' screamed Ethel, dropping the

53

rope and her clinging dentures with it as she spoke. Before continuing, she picked her dentures up from the ground, wiped the compost and beetle corpses from them, and placed them back inside her mouth. 'What's happening here? You never tell me anything!'

'Well,' Charlie started to explain again, 'if you stand up straight like that for the next couple of hours....'

'I'm not doing this for two hours! You know you only pay me to do the housework!'

'It's for your Queen and country,' Charlie offered, hopefully.

'The Queen?' Thoughts of an OBE and an invitation to the royal garden party flashed through Ethel's mind. 'I can just picture it,' she fantasised. 'Me, a lowly maid, a hit with the royals—sipping tea with their royalnesses on a hot summer day while nattering to Fergie about my humble beginnings as a gentlemen's lavatory attendant in Birmingham.'

'All right then,' she gave in, her mind made up. 'What do I have to do?'

'Good,' said Charlie. 'I knew I could rely on you. You just stay there until the Clothes Line Snatcher strikes. Then, when he approaches, you smash him one on the bonce and then we've caught him.'

But won't he notice me?'

'Not really,' said Charlie, defending his scheme. 'You're about as thin as a post, and as long as you wear a dark brown overcoat and pretend you've got woodworm then everything will be okay.'

'May I enquire what *you* will be doing all this time?' Ethel asked suspiciously.

'I will be hiding behind that bush,' Charlie answered, pointing to a far corner of the garden. 'If the Clothes Line Snatcher shoots you or anything, don't worry—I will be right there behind that bush.'

'Shoots me? That sounds painful. Crumbs!'

Ethel impersonated a clothes line post for about one-and-a-half hours, being careful not to move an inch in case she was found out. She was frightened, but she kept reassuring herself with the fact that her boss was watching from behind that bush in the furthest corner of the garden, eager and ready to protect her if anything happened.

'Snore.' Charlie was sleeping behind the bush.

Then, after all this waiting, Ethel saw some movement out of the corners of her eyes. It was the dreaded Clothes Line Snatcher climbing over the wooden fence of the garden, continually looking back over both of his shoulders to make sure no one was watching him.

'Hee hee hee!' he cackled in a very criminal-sounding voice. 'At last I'm here in Charlie Digestives' back garden, and now I can do something that I've wanted to do for years!'

'Help!' thought Ethel, sweating, even though it was a typically cold British day. 'It's him! It's the Clothes Line Snatcher! I'm terrifically frightened, you know. Gasp and gulp!'

The Clothes Line Snatcher (or the Snatcher as he was often referred to) was wearing striped, criminal-looking clothes, and he also had a black hood over his white furry head, with two small holes for his poodle eyes to see through. No one had ever seen the face under this hood (except for himself, of course), so no one knew who the Clothes Line Snatcher really was. He was holding a sack that he put all his stolen clothes lines in, and there was a scabbard at his side that contained a black umbrella.

He took this umbrella from the scabbard and quietly tiptoed up to Charlie Digestives' clothes line. He flicked a switch built into the handle, and a sharp blade immediately appeared at the other end.

'Crumbs!' Ethel felt like fainting, but she stayed perfectly still and hoped that the Snatcher had not seen through her surprisingly effective disguise.

The Snatcher neatly chopped one end of the clothes line from the wooden post it was attached to, then walked over to Ethel's side, winding the line round his fist as he went.

'Great!' he said. 'One more slice and then it's over, and Charlie will no longer have a clothes line to hang all his washing on. Boy, will he ever be sorry for all the times he's tried to thwart my schemes.'

The Snatcher lifted his umbrella/knife just a few millimetres away from Ethel's nose, and after a few seconds of vicious hacking his task was finished. As he bent down to deposit the length of rope in his clothes line sack, Ethel spat the remaining piece of clothes line from her mouth and raised her paw to bash her dreaded enemy on the head. But as he unexpectedly turned back round, she quickly dropped her poodle arm back by her side.

'Fantastic!' said the Clothes Line Snatcher, and as he flung the sack over his shoulder to climb back over the garden fence, Ethel took a bright shining police whistle from her pocket and blew it as hard as she could. The piercing sound of the whistle woke Charlie, and he jumped, startled, out of the bush.

'Owch, those stinging nettles,' he groaned as he pulled himself up from the cluster of offensive plants he had just landed on. He rubbed his aching poodle skin, then shouted to Ethel: 'Quick! After him!'

The shocked Clothes Line Snatcher turned round and realised that he was being chased.

'Lummee!' he cursed. 'Trust this to happen. Charlie Digestives must have been on to me.'

He dropped his sack so that he could run faster, then Charlie followed him on a frantic hurdles chase of back garden fences. Ethel pulled up her skirt and attempted a feeble scissor jump over the three-foot high barrier.

'Eek!' She stood up from her next-door-neighbour's pond and wiped the water and croaking amphibians from her overcoat. Then she resumed her chase for the Clothes Line Snatcher.

'You won't escape me,' shouted Charlie, 'you fiend, you!'

The Snatcher ignored Charlie's rude remarks and continued to leap over the seemingly never-ending line of back garden fences. He soon jumped over the final fence and found himself on a near-deserted Walbridge street. Thinking quickly, he confiscated a rusty pair of roller skates from a pimply six-year-old poodle who was passing him, and hid round a nearby street corner to put them on hurriedly.

'Waah!' screamed the poodle, running to tell his mummy. 'Big poodle steal my skates! Me angry! Me go poo poo plops!'

'Now, now, Simon dear. There's no need to be rude.'

'Good!' said the Clothes Line Snatcher as he sped away on the skates. 'Now Charlie Digestives will never be able to catch me!'

But Charlie had also realised that he needed a faster method of transportation. Somewhere along his travels he found a unicycle, and he was trying his best to pedal along. He had never used a unicycle before, and he was having a lot of trouble—he kept losing his balance and overturning. But despite all these problems, he was determined to catch up with the Snatcher.

Ethel overtook Charlie on a pogo stick she had borrowed from someone's back garden. She was quite an expert at pogoing, and she actually came second in the 1926 Kellogg's Corn Flakes International Pogo Stick Championship. She didn't realise, however, that the pogo stick had just been treated to a fresh coat of paint. As the paint dried, her legs and poodle fur were sticking to the metal.

The Clothes Line Snatcher was racing along the road at ninety miles an hour. A police car was chasing him because he was speeding.

Just a bit further up the road, a very old female poodle in a wheelchair was trying to cross the road.

'If only some nice kind poodle would push me along,' she wished out loud. Her wish was soon answered.

Kerthump!

She was now travelling at ninety miles an hour, thanks to the Clothes Line Snatcher who was holding on to the back of her wheelchair.

'Thank you, young poodle,' she said gratefully, looking over her shoulder. 'As well as helping me cross the road, you're taking me to my old poodle's home.' She opened her handbag and dipped a trembling paw inside. 'Here, have ten pee,' the poodle pensioner generously offered. 'You deserve it.'

'Er...no thanks,' refused the Snatcher, who had more important things on his mind at the moment than ten pence pieces. 'Please, no....'

But the old poodle persisted. 'No, I insist,' she

said, and she continued to search for the loose change in her bag.

Suddenly, for no reason at all (except perhaps for the fact that the steering was faulty on his unicycle), Charlie left the rest of the racers and turned round a corner into a small side road.

'Help!' he cried. 'I can't control this thing!' There was no brake on the unicycle, and he did not want to jump off because he had fallen from it too many times already (as evidenced by his heavily bruised poodle knees) and he knew the painful consequences if he did. He could not steer the thing either, so he just had to rely on the will of the one-wheeled vehicle and hope that nothing too terrible happened.

As he road unsteadily along, he noticed a sign by the side of the road that he had not seen before in Walbridge.

'I wonder what it says,' he thought, and he slowly read it out loud. 'The...Annual...British...Hang-Gliding...Championship...Half...A...Mile... Ahead....' Then he repeated the words as they registered in his brain. 'Oh, the Annual British Hang-Gliding Championship Half-A-Mile Ahead.' That should be fun.'

He accelerated past the sign and continued uni-cycling towards the site of the championship.

8

Professor Alfred Boggles *did* make it to the Walbridge Museum in time, and there was complete silence as he stepped onto the stage of the museum's lecture hall. The room was only built to seat 500 poodles, but there was almost twice as many in there: journalists, photographers, television cameramen, distinguished scientists from all over the world, and different inhabitants of Walbridge, including about a hundred young poodles from Heathlands Secondary School. All were excited at what they were about to see, and all had been making a tremendous din in there, chattering away to each other about all the different implications of the 'Wow' Screen. One of the television cameramen who didn't have anyone to talk to had been loudly singing Christmas carols because he felt he should somehow contribute towards all the noise. But now there was quiet as the professor walked up to the microphone. Everyone was eager to hear what he had to say.

'Goodt mornink, ladeez undt chentlemen!' Professor Alfred Boggles shouted into the microphone.

'Good morning, Professor Alfred Boggles!' everyone cheerfully shouted back in unison.

Alfred looked a typical loony professor. The grey poodle hair on his head stuck straight up in the air as if he had just got out of bed after a restless night and hadn't bothered to comb it. He had a long flowing beard—much of that sticking straight up in the air as well—and also a handlebar moustache which curled round and round at the ends. He wore thick round glasses that made his eyes look three times bigger than normal, and a white laboratory coat with different coloured stains on it: ketchup stains, egg stains and goodness-knows-what-else stains. The professor was quite tall as well, but of course you don't have to be tall to be a loony professor. Alfred was the founder of the LPS-GB (the Loony Professors Society of Great Britain), and many of his colleagues in this society were in the audience this morning.

'Before I start, let me chust thank you all for cummink here diss mornink.'

'Atishoo!' went Emily Wardrobe, a sixty-nine-year-old female bricklayer who was sitting on the front row.

'Bless you,' said everyone else in the audience, but the professor said 'Gesundheit!' instead because he liked being different. Then he continued: 'I am sure you all are dyink to see der "Vow" Screen. But first, let me chust explain vot led up to der invention off diss device.'

The audience gasped when the professor held up the official promotional poster for the latest James Bond film. Emily Wardrobe didn't gasp because she was too busy blowing her nose. But she made up for this later by gasping twice at the next suitable opportunity. The reason the audience gasped was that the James Bond on the poster was slightly different from the James Bond they were used to. Instead of the canine features of the hunky Timothy Dalmation staring out at them, there was one of those human beings dressed up in the same type of suit that James Bond usually wore and holding the same sort of gun. The glamorous female on the poster was also a human being instead of a dog.

'It looks strange, dussn't it?' said the professor.

'Yes,' agreed Emily Wardrobe, 'it looks very strange indeed. Very strange indeed it is. It's very very....'

'Shut up, and let Professor Boggles get on with it!' shouted a journalist who was sitting in the audience, and he threw a bicycle pump at her that he just happened to have with him. Emily started making rude noises with this, but Alfred tried to ignore her and proceeded with his explanation.

'Two years ago I started ecksperimentink with different methods off time travel.'

'Parmph!' went the bicycle pump.

'Von off der ideas I played around vith voss a time travellink Rice Krispies packet.' The professor pointed to a family-size Rice Krispies packet on the table next to him. The packet was empty (the professor had eaten all of the Rice Krispies beforehand—all in the name of scientific research, of course), and it was hooked up to all sorts of impressive-looking electrical wires, many of which were there for no other reason than to look impressive.

'Phssht,' continued the bicycle pump.

'It's becoss off diss Rice Krispies packet dat I got der strange Chames Bondt poster. Let me show you all how it vorks.' The professor produced another movie poster from underneath the table, this time of *Superdog—The Movie*. He carefully folded this in half, then in half again, and so on, and so on, until it was small enough to fit inside the Rice Krispies packet. Then he dropped it inside and pressed a large green button on the table.

Lots of dramatic things started happening. Sparks seemed to shoot up all the wires into the Rice Krispies packet, the packet started glowing all sorts of funny colours, and seven male ballet dancers in extremely tight costumes started dancing enthusiastically across the stage. As soon as they reached the table with the Rice Krispies packet they stopped, some of them looking puzzled and the others looking very embarrassed indeed.

'Crumbs,' went Rodney, puffing at his pipe because he was the world's only pipe-smoking ballet dancer. 'We must have gone through the wrong stage door. This is the lecture hall in the museum. *We* want the Walbridge Opera House next door.'

'Sorry, everyone,' Rodney apologised to Professor Alfred Boggles and the audience. And then he led his six comrades in an energetic dance back across the stage, doing an impressive pirouette along the way while still smoking his pipe.

But Rodney's apology fell on deaf ears. No one in the lecture hall heard it, and no one, in fact, had even noticed the strange entrance and sudden exit of the ballet dancers. Every eye in that lecture hall was staring intently at the Rice Krispies packet, glowing brighter and brighter with every passing second as more sparkling crackles and pops shot through the wires. Even Emily Wardrobe was staring intently at the packet, which explained why no one had heard any rude noises from the bicycle pump for the last few minutes.

Eventually all the crackling and popping (and other electrical-type stuff) stopped, and Professor Alfred Boggles retrieved the movie poster from the Rice Krispies packet. He quickly unfolded it, and without even looking at it he held it up for the audience to see.

'Gasp,' went the audience, and Emily Wardrobe gasped twice, making up for her negligence the last time.

The superhero on the poster was now a man instead of a poodle, and instead of saying *Superdog— The Movie* it now said *Superman—The Movie*.

'Diss iss exactly vot happened ven I first used diss time travellink Rice Krispies packet,' the professor explained. 'Vot I vonted voss for der poster to travel three hours into der future. But it didn't travel in time at all. Instead, it seemed to travel into anudder universe—a parallel universe vere human beinks are der dominant species on earth, and vere der star off *Superdog—Der Movie* iss a man instead off a poodle.'

There were a number of sceptics in the audience. One of them was Mr Bright Spark from Cambridge University who stood up and protested: 'But that *Superman* poster doesn't prove anything. For all we know, you could have hired an artist to paint a fake poster, and hidden it in the Rice Krispies packet before we all came in.'

Emily Wardrobe gasped again, then blushed because she realised that this wasn't the right time to gasp.

The professor defended himself against Mr Bright Spark's accusation. 'I am vell avare dat diss poster iss not adequate evidence off der existence off udder universes.' He laid the poster down on the table and walked over to a mysterious tall object covered in a white sheet at the centre of the stage. 'Dat iss vy for der last two years I haff been vorkink on a device dat dussn't chust brink back objects from udder universes—but actually shows uss vot iss goink on dere. Last veek I finally succeeded in my aim.' The professor slowly pulled the white sheet away from the tall object. 'Ladeez undt chentlemen,' he dramatically announced, 'I present to you...der "Vow" Screen!'

Half of the audience went wild with excitement at

this point, screaming, shouting 'Wow' and loudly clapping their paws—and the lonely television cameraman enthusiastically sang 'Climb Every Mountain' because it seemed suitably triumphant. The other half of the audience remained perfectly silent, not at all sure what all the fuss was about. They hadn't made out a word the professor had said, which is perfectly understandable because Professor Alfred Boggles *does* have a very strange accent. But this mystified half of the audience soon became excited as well when the professor turned the 'Wow' Screen on.

The 'Wow' Screen was one of those large video screens that only pop stars and very rich people (and *very* loony professors) have. But this video screen didn't show just ordinary television programmes. The professor had cleverly adapted it to show what was going on in other universes. Right now it was displaying a picture of a Walbridge Museum lecture hall full of larger-than-normal snails in the audience. To those in the poodle universe, it was like they were looking at a mirror image of themselves, except that they saw themselves as snails on the 'Wow' Screen instead of poodles. The picture was remarkably clear, and the poodles looked astonished. The snails on the screen looked astonished as well because, like the poodles, they were discovering for the first time that there were other universes as well as their own.

'As you can see,' explained the professor, 'der universe vee are observink iss von vere snails are der main inhabitants off planet earth. Vot you are seeink iss happenink right now in deir universe.'

The professor took a remote control unit from one of the pockets of his laboratory coat. 'Der snail universe issn't der only universe dat can be seen on der

"Vow" Screen.' He aimed the remote control unit at the screen and pressed a few buttons on it.

'Diss iss der kangaroo universe,' the professor announced when the picture on the screen changed to one of kangaroos sitting in the Walbridge Museum lecture hall.

'Now der Terry Vogan universe,' said the professor, pressing more buttons on his remote control unit. The screen then showed a lecture hall full of beings that looked exactly like the poodle version of Terry Wogan.

'And finally, der human beink universe.' The professor pressed two more buttons so that the picture on the screen contained hundreds of astonished human beings, sitting in the Walbridge Museum lecture hall of *our* universe.

Mr Bright Spark from Cambridge University stood up again. 'All these images on your "Wow" Screen don't necessarily prove that there are other universes,' he challenged. 'What you're showing us now could just be a specially prepared video tape, with puppets or special effects. How can you prove that what we're seeing is live—actually happening at this very moment in a "human being universe"?'

The professor turned to face Mr Bright Spark. 'I perfectly understandt all your doubts,' he calmly responded. 'After all, vot vee are dealink vith here iss so mind-bogglinkly extraordinary dat you *do* haff to be careful not chust to believe der claims off any old professor—especially a loony professor like me. You must haff absolute, incontrovertible proof. So dat iss vy I will now ask for two volunteers from der audience to help me prove vunce and for all dat vot you are seeink on my "Vow" Screen cannot possibly be pre-recorded.'

Everyone in the audience immediately shot one paw up in the air to volunteer, including Mr Bright Spark. The television cameraman was so eager to volunteer that he put up *two* paws, *and* one of his hind legs. But he soon fell painfully backwards because it's very hard to balance on just one leg.

Eventually the professor picked two pupils from Heathlands Secondary School: a male (Jonathan Matthews) and a female (Penny Green). He motioned for them both to join him on the stage, and they eagerly complied, their hearts beating very fast because they were excited.

They couldn't believe their luck—but they weren't lucky at all. Little did they, or anyone else in the lecture hall, realise that the events of the next few minutes would plunge them both head-first into a year-long nightmare of horrific proportions.

Gasp. It's so awful, I can hardly bear to write about it.

'Blurp!' went the bicycle pump.

9

Those outside on the road were still zooming along at incredible speeds. Ethel was jumping up and down on her pogo stick like crazy, and she hadn't noticed the sudden disappearance of Charlie Digestives down the small side road. She was almost three-quarters-of-a-mile in front of the police car.

'You'd better take it easy on the speed,' cautioned the policepoodle who wasn't driving.

'Why?' wondered the other policepoodle, eating two Crunchies simultaneously with the paw that wasn't on the steering wheel.

'Well, there's a downward slope just ahead that leads straight to the Walbridge Museum,' he explained, 'and if we aren't careful we'll crash into it.'

'Don't worry,' the driving policepoodle reassured his colleague. He quickly finished his Crunchies, then took a tub of strawberry-flavoured ice cream from underneath his helmet. 'I know what I'm doing.'

Charlie Digestives was causing havoc in the refreshment tent of the hang-gliding championship. He had no control over his unicycle and he kept knocking things over, including fellow poodles. Luckily, the two home-made chipboard tables, the tin of custard creams and Gladys' imitation fruit salad hat (along with Gladys herself), had been insured.

'Help! There's a mad poodle on the loose!' screamed Doreen, Gladys' best friend, who was desperately trying to escape from the all-seeing wheel of the unibike.

'Good morning, Madam,' went Charlie, politely. He couldn't raise his hat to her because he wasn't wearing one, so he saluted instead. Then he ran her over.

'Whoops,' he went. He was now heading for the starting position just six inches away from the edge of a tall hill.

'Oh no, I'll fall over the side if I don't stop soon,' said Charlie. (Actually, he didn't say this at all because he was too busy panicking. But I decided to put it in because it's nice and dramatic, and it cleverly explains what's going on.) Luckily his unicycle ran over a large stone and Charlie somersaulted through the air.

'Oomph!' he went when he landed on the ground.

As soon as he had regained his breath he peered over the side of the hill, just in time to see the unicycle smashing into the rocky ground far below. Charlie gulped when he saw the mangled ex-unicycle and realised that it could have been him down there as well. Then he looked round to try and find another form of transport to help him catch up with the runaway Clothes Line Snatcher.

The first thing he saw was an unattended hang-glider just a few feet away from him. He quickly strapped it on, hoping that the owner wouldn't mind him borrowing it. Then he raced forward and bravely leaped over the side of the hill.

'Hey, wait a minute!' shouted a concerned observer, spraying half-digested lumps of jammy doughnut on another observer next to him. 'There might not be enough wind! Oops! Sorry about that, me old mate. Here's a hankie to take that jam out of your eyes.'

But it was too late. Charlie had already jumped.

'Aaaaaahh!' He was heading straight for the ground, and he wished that he hadn't been so hasty in his decision to jump.

'Aaaaaahh!' he screamed again because he was *very* frightened.

Then he screamed: 'Aaaaaardvaark!' because he thought it would make a clever change from 'Aaaaaahh!'

Luckily, he didn't have to scream for much longer. Just as he was about to crash-land on some extremely prickly bushes, a sudden gust of wind blew the hang-glider upwards and Charlie found himself floating gracefully through the air.

'Wow! This is fantastic!' he said, and he carefully steered his way back to the main road in Walbridge.

The Clothes Line Snatcher nervously gasped when he realised that he was roller skating down a steep road with the Walbridge Museum at the end of it.

'I think I'll get off here now,' said the female old poodle as she sighted her old poodles' home just ahead. The Snatcher obligingly let go of the wheel-chair and let her steer her way back to her home at ninety miles an hour.

'He-elp!' wailed Ethel when she saw the Wal-bridge Museum just ahead. She was jumping much too fast to stop, and she wasn't looking forward to bashing into the front of the museum.

Meanwhile, the two policepoodles in the police car had just discovered that their brakes weren't working.

Totally unaware of all the chaos on the roads out-side, Professor Alfred Boggles continued with his demonstration of the 'Wow' Screen in the Walbridge Museum lecture hall. The professor told Jonathan Matthews and Penny Green to stand in front of the screen, which was still receiving live pictures from the human universe.

'Wow!' went Jonathan and Penny when they had done as he said, facing towards the screen and seeing the human versions of themselves staring back at them. Everyone in the audience went 'Wow' as well, including the no-longer sceptical Mr Bright Spark from Cambridge University.

The professor smiled smugly to himself at every-one's reaction. He knew that everyone would say

'Wow!' when they saw what his screen could do, and that, of course, is why he had called it the 'Wow' Screen.

The poodle Jonathan Matthews put his paw over his mouth in shock, and the human Jonathan on the screen put his hand over his mouth at exactly the same time.

The poodle Penny Green laughed nervously because she wasn't sure what else to do, and the human Penny on the screen laughed nervously as well.

The poodle Jonathan decided to have some fun with this, so he started jumping up and down on the stage like an excited gorilla, making appropriate gorilla noises to go with his impression. The human Jonathan on the screen did likewise.

'Ooka ooka,' they went, both of them sounding very convincing (although those in the poodle universe could only hear the poodle Jonathan Matthews as the 'Wow' Screen didn't transmit sound).

The poodle Penny followed Jonathan's example and began singing a song by pop-star Madogga to see if her human equivalent on the screen would do the same. She did, and they both strummed imaginary guitars while they sang.

'Wow!' went Jonathan and Penny again.

'Wow!' repeated everyone in the audience.

And Professor Boggles continued to smile contentedly. You could tell that he was enjoying himself.

Charlie Digestives was enjoying himself as well. He had never flown with a hang-glider before, and he felt quite exhilarated—so exhilarated in fact that he hadn't noticed he'd been slowly descending and was about to crash into the back of the Walbridge Museum.

'Oops,' he went when he suddenly saw where he was heading, and he steered himself upwards just in time. Soon he was flying above the main road leading down to the *front* of the museum.

'Brill!' he said when he saw the Clothes Line Snatcher and the others approaching him. 'It's them! What perfect timing!'

Back inside the museum, Professor Alfred Boggles wasn't smiling contentedly any more. Instead, he looked very concerned. A fight had broken out between Emily Wardrobe and the journalist who'd thrown the bicycle pump at her, and there was chaos in the lecture hall.

After everyone had said 'Wow!' for the second time, Emily had resumed her rude-noise-making activities with the pump. The journalist couldn't stand much more of this, so he had made his way to the front row while angrily fuming ('Fume,' he went), and his clenched right paw had applied severe pressure to the lower region of her face. (He smashed her one on the gob, for those readers who are less technically minded.) The two then started wrestling on the floor, and the audience began cheering for one or the other. Half of the audience shouted, 'Emily! Emily!' because they wanted Emily Wardrobe to win, and the other half shouted, 'Journalist! Journalist!' because, of course, they were on the journalist's side. People started betting, and a lot of money changed hands (or paws) over the eventual outcome of the fight.

Soon Professor Alfred Boggles decided to intervene. He resented this interruption of his important demonstration, and he wanted everyone's attention to return to him and his screen as soon as possible.

'Stop it, you zwei...I mean, you two,' he

72

demanded, jumping from the stage and pulling the two wrestlers up from the ground, one with his right paw and the other with his left. As well as being a genius, Professor Alfred Boggles was apparently quite a strongman. 'I hate seeink violence, especially durink von off my demonstrations!'

'Oof!' went the journalist, winded after being lifted so suddenly into the air. Professor Boggles was holding him by his collar, and his two lower paws were three inches off the ground.

'Let me at him!' screamed Emily Wardrobe, also suspended in the air by Professor Boggles. She was kicking and punching, and struggling to break free.

'As you vish, Madam,' said Alfred. 'Diss iss a free country, undt you undt diss chentleman are perfectly entitled to senselessly beat der livink daylights out off each udder, if dat iss vot you both vont.' Alfred strode down the aisle of the lecture hall, dragging the two of them along the floor behind him. 'However,' he insisted, 'I must ask dat you resume your violent activities outside so dat I can continue showink people my "Vow" Screen.'

Professor Boggles left the doors of the lecture hall open behind him as he dragged the two into the museum's foyer. Then he left them happily fighting each other by the souvenir postcard stands as he went to open the creaky museum doors.

'Golly undt crikey!' he said when the doors had been opened and a criminal-looking figure on roller skates shot straight past him and on towards the lecture hall. 'Vot on earth voss dat?'

'Aaaaaah!' screamed the Clothes Line Snatcher as he found himself shooting down the aisle of the lecture hall and heading straight for the 'Wow' Screen on the stage.

Professor Boggles shrugged his shoulders and was just about to roll the two wrestlers outside when another strange figure brushed past him. This time it was a breathless old poodle on a pogo stick.

'H-he-elp m-me!' Ethel stuttered, her desperate voice echoing round the foyer of the Walbridge Museum. 'I c-can-an't st-sto-op j-jump-p-ping!' This was true, unfortunately, and she reluctantly pogoed into the lecture hall and on towards the stage.

Professor Boggles scratched his head in amazement. On the floor behind him Emily Wardrobe scratched the *journalist*'s head, and the journalist retaliated by pulling off her wig. They hadn't noticed all the excitement going on around them because they were still busy fighting.

'Whooooosh!' went the next thing that came through the doorway of the museum. It *flew* through, to be more precise, a large hang-glider with a frightened detective strapped to it. Charlie Digestives had steered the hang-glider round 180 degrees outside so that he could catch up with the Clothes Line Snatcher.

'Help!' Charlie screamed when he saw that the hang-glider was about to smash into the wall next to the lecture hall entrance. 'I'm going to...'

Kerthump! Scrunch!

'...crash.'

The crumpled ex-hang-glider was now blocking the entrance to the lecture hall. Charlie Digestives, still strapped to it, lay dazed on the ground. He had thumped his head on the hard wall of the foyer before the hang-glider's premature descent, and he groaned in time to the imaginary stars that were whirring around in the air above his throbbing bonce.

74

His groans were soon drowned out by another crash, this one much louder and more powerful because it came from the police car smashing sideways into the entrance of the Walbridge Museum at ninety miles an hour. (The car had swerved before impact, and that was why it was in a sideways position.)

'Keeeeerrraashh!' it went, with bricks falling everywhere, and Professor Boggles went, 'Goodtness!' because he wasn't quite sure what to make of all this sudden activity. He cautiously stepped forward to examine the highly-mangled police car—the left-hand side of it in the foyer, and the right-hand side outside—then looked up when he heard two puffing poodles climbing over the top of the car and into the museum. It was the two policepoodles, and they were relatively unhurt because they had both jumped out of the car just seconds before the crash.

'Sorry about the mess, prof,' said one of the policepoodles when they'd made it into the foyer. He lifted his helmet apologetically.

The other policepoodle lifted his helmet as well, but for a different reason. He was hungry (as usual), and he was reaching for the box of Chicken McNuggets that was under there.

Inside the lecture hall, Jonathan Matthews and Penny Green were frozen in shock on the stage at the strange figures heading straight for them. The helpless Clothes Line Snatcher lost his balance as he roller skated over the bicycle pump that had been left on the floor, and he somersaulted upwards and onto the stage. He then found himself skating towards the 'Wow' Screen.

'Urk!' he went, not looking forward to his sure-to-be painful impact with this daunting device. Thinking quickly, he pulled the umbrella from the scabbard at his side and flicked the switch that opened it out. He thrust the umbrella in front of him, hoping that it would soften his impact with the screen, but unfortunately all it did was push Penny and Jonathan forward so that three poodles were now heading for the 'Wow' Screen instead of just the Snatcher.

'I want my mummy!' screamed the Clothes Line Snatcher, and Jonathan and Penny screamed as well.

Something strange happened at this point. Instead of the three of them smacking into the screen, they somehow disappeared inside it. This strange disappearance was immediately followed by an almighty explosion with sparks and bits of the 'Wow' Screen flying everywhere, and dark smoke rising from the remains of the screen. A few split seconds later there was an unearthly sucking sound as the screen mysteriously reconstructed itself and all the sparks and smoke were sucked back inside. The three were then belched back out of it before it finally collapsed on the stage in a thousand-or-so pieces, screws and bolts rolling away from it and the screen itself completely ripped to shreds because of all the jumping in and out of it. It looked almost beyond repair.

Jonathan and Penny lay unconscious on the stage. Whatever had happened to them inside the 'Wow' Screen had obviously been too much for them.

The Clothes Line Snatcher wasn't unconscious, but he was obviously in a deep state of shock. Still clutching his umbrella, he groaned for a while on the stage then looked up to see where he was. He gasped when he saw hundreds of poodles staring back at him, and he gasped even more when he looked down and saw that he was a poodle himself.

'I'm getting out of this freaky place,' the Snatcher

announced, much fear and confusion in his voice. He closed the umbrella and stuffed it back inside his scabbard, then jumped from the stage and roller skated back down the aisle. Ethel had reluctantly been jumping up and down in the aisle the last few moments because her legs were stuck to the now-dry paint on the pogo stick, and she was violently knocked down by the Snatcher as he skated past her.

'Ow-wow-wowch!' she stuttered on the floor. 'That h-hurt!'

The next person the Snatcher knocked over was Charlie Digestives in the foyer. Charlie had just summoned up enough energy to stand up, with what was left of the hang-glider hanging feebly from his back.

'Oof!' went Charlie as the Snatcher pushed him out of the way, and he fell painfully backwards, crushing the hang-glider even more.

The Clothes Line Snatcher, without stopping to apologise (what a nasty poodle he was), frantically scrambled over the police car that was blocking the entrance to the museum, then roller skated away to goodness-knows-where in Walbridge.

'Just a minute,' said one of the policepoodles in the foyer. 'Wasn't that the Clothes Line Snatcher who just went past us?'

'I don't know,' said the other policepoodle, 'but these are jolly good Chicken McNuggets. Burp!'

Professor Boggles stood silently in the foyer, deep in thought. So much had happened these last few seconds—too much for him to take in immediately. He replayed the recent events in his mind, then remembered that he'd heard an explosion from inside the lecture hall.

'Mein "Vow" Screen!' he exclaimed, thinking that maybe his precious 'Wow' Screen was something to do with the explosion. Worriedly he ran into the lecture hall to see if his suspicions were correct.

10

Things were just as chaotic in the Walbridge Museum of the *human* planet earth. The 'Wow' Screen of the human Professor Boggles had also exploded, and the unconscious bodies of Jonathan and Penny on the lecture hall stage were human instead of poodle. In fact, everything on the human planet earth had happened exactly the same as on the poodle earth, except that it had happened to the human versions of people instead of their poodle selves.

Professor Boggles accidentally knocked the human Charlie Digestives backwards as he ran into the Walbridge Museum lecture hall. (Charlie had just stood up again after being pushed over by the Clothes Line Snatcher.) Then the professor raced up the aisle, knocking the human Ethel over (who had also just got up again), and expertly leaped onto the stage. He cried when he saw the remains of the 'Wow' Screen in front of him, a mess of melted wires, scorched silicon chips, mangled plastic casing, and an almost unrecognisable screen that looked as if it had been ripped in about three million places. If the screen was still working it would have shown an astonished poodle audience, completely stunned silent and not at all sure what to make of all the sudden activity and the strange destruction of the 'Wow' Screen. But, of course, the screen *wasn't* still working, and it looked as if it would be years before Professor Boggles would be able to get it back into perfect working order.

'Sob,' went the professor. 'Mein "Vow" Screen—destroyed! Two years' vork, completely down der proverbial drain!' (As you can see, the human Professor Boggles *also* had an extremely strange accent.)

The professor sobbed a bit more, and he sniffed a few times as well for variety.

'Sob. Sniff. Sob,' he went.

He soon heard two people behind him jumping onto the stage. One was Charlie Digestives, who had finally managed to unstrap the remains of the hang-glider from his back. The other was Ethel, jumping up and down like crazy because it was the only way she could stay upright while stuck to the pogo stick.

Charlie looked dazed from all his falls to the ground. His head was still throbbing, and he was also exhausted from all the unicycling and hang-gliding outside. But Charlie Digestives was a world-famous detective with important work to do, and tough world-famous detectives don't let trivial things like throbbing heads and exhaustion stop them from carrying out their duties. He placed a comforting hand on Professor Boggles' shoulder, smiled sympathetically at him, then went to inspect the unconscious bodies of Jonathan Matthews and Penny Green.

Penny was groaning when Charlie knelt down beside her, and he slowly helped her to sit up. She opened her eyes to see where she was...and then she stopped groaning.

'Gasp,' she went. (It's very hard to gasp and groan at the same time, and that is why she stopped groaning.) 'This place is full of human beings wearing clothes.' Her eyes wide open in shock, she turned to look at Charlie and gasped again. 'You're a human being too.' She then looked down at herself, and she was horrified with what she saw. 'And I...I'm a human as well.' She hesitated for a few split seconds, not quite sure what to do. Then—her mind obviously made up—she fainted.

The thump of her falling to the ground woke Jonathan up. He too was helped by Charlie to sit up slowly, and he rubbed his tired watery eyes to see where he was.

'Eh?' he said when he noticed that there was no fur on his paws (which were now human hands). He felt around under his shirt with one of these hands and realised that the rest of him was relatively hairless as well. 'I...I've turned into a human being!' he exclaimed, a look of utter desperation on his face. 'This shouldn't be! I'm a poodle—not a human!' He gasped and groaned very nearly at the same time. Then he fainted, lying next to Penny again on the stage.

Charlie thoughtfully looked down at Penny and Jonathan and realised what must have happened. He knew that the 'Wow' Screen could show what was happening in other universes (Professor Boggles was a good friend of Charlie's who kept him informed of all his experiments), and he guessed that when Penny, Jonathan and the Snatcher crashed through the screen, their human souls (or whatever it was that made them thinking creatures with a conscience) must have entered the bodies of their poodle selves in the poodle universe, and vice-versa. The

Penny and Jonathan on the stage must be the poodle Penny and Jonathan in the bodies of their human counterparts. And roller skating around Walbridge right now was the poodle version of the Clothes Line Snatcher in the body of a human being.

Charlie tried to imagine what the three of them must feel like, trapped in bodies that weren't their own and finding themselves in a world where everyone was different from them. They were a long, long way from home—a whole universe away. What a strange and lonely place it must be for them.

'I felt the same, you know, when I came to earth once as a human to set a few things right.'

'Huh? Who said that?'

Charlie looked up and saw a smiling figure in a white robe standing directly in front of him. His smile was so penetrating that Charlie could feel it in his bones. His whole face seemed to glow with kindness. And Charlie could see the universe in his eyes.

'Who are you?' he asked, trembling slightly because he felt like he was in the presence of some kind of king or prime minister. But the man disappeared before the words had even left his mouth, and Charlie saw instead Emily Wardrobe and the journalist she'd been wrestling with (the human versions of them) running hand-in-hand up the aisle of the lecture hall. Both of them jumped onto the stage, and Emily Wardrobe made a special announcement.

'Cough cough,' she went, loudly clearing her throat (which is what all good speakers do before they make a special announcement), and she went on to explain that while she and the journalist had been fighting in the foyer they'd realised how much they loved each other.

'So,' the journalist continued for her (he didn't

loudly clear his throat before he said this, so he obviously wasn't a good speaker), 'Emily and I are now engaged to be married.'

Emily and the journalist smiled, and their smiles were so unusually radiant that no one noticed all the dark gaps between their teeth, and all the scratches and bruises on their faces from all the fighting they'd been doing.

Everyone in the audience smiled as well, and they all stood up to give the happy couple a rousing round of applause. Ethel smiled as she merrily continued pogoing up and down (she liked soppy things like this), and even the poor professor managed a feeble grin as he momentarily forgot the untimely demise of his 'Wow' Screen.

But Charlie didn't smile at all. He had too many things on his mind.

Charlie was a very sensitive detective, and he felt sad for Jonathan and Penny. Even worse, he felt totally frustrated because there didn't seem to be anything he could do to help. The 'Wow' Screen was destroyed, and there was no way they could get back to their universe until Professor Boggles had rebuilt it. That could take years, and even then there was no guaranteeing that the 'Wow' Screen could get them home.

Also—and this was the thing that was *most* on Charlie's mind—he was confused about that mysterious figure in the robe. Why was it that no one else seemed to have seen him? And why did he disappear so suddenly?

Charlie felt so good when the figure was there— totally loved and accepted, something he wasn't used to. It was similar to that comforting feeling he experienced in his bedroom first thing this morning:

that some powerful being, who loved everyone very much, was sorting out all the problems of the world. Charlie wondered if that being could help Jonathan and Penny with *their* problems.

'Naah,' he eventually sighed, realising he was being unrealistic. It would almost take a miracle to get Jonathan and Penny back where they belonged, and miracles didn't happen any more, did they?

Charlie tried to smile then so that he didn't look too out of place with the others in the lecture hall.

But the smile wasn't at all convincing.

* * *

'And all of that happened just over a year ago,' said the poodle Penny Green in human form, finishing off her story to a bewildered Dickie Dustbin in the Heathlands tuck shop room. 'Right now in the poodle universe, the human versions of the Clothes Line Snatcher, Jonathan Matthews and me, are trapped in poodle bodies. And similarly, the poodle versions of ourselves are trapped here in *human* bodies.

'Professor Boggles has been busy reconstructing his "Wow" Screen since then so that he can attempt to get us back to the poodle universe, and bring our human selves back here. But the "Wow" Screen is such a complicated contraption that he still hasn't finished. To be honest with you, I seriously doubt that we'll *ever* get home.'

'So you and Jonathan are not...?'

'That's right,' answered Penny, anticipating Dickie's question. 'We're not in love at all, but we stick together all the time because we need each other's support in these strange surroundings. The only other people who know about us really being poodles are our parents—the human versions of them, that is. They've been helping us to adjust, while the professor works on his "Wow" Screen and while Charlie Digestives continues to try and find the Clothes Line Snatcher.'

Another question from Dickie: 'What about the Clothes Line Snatcher? Where is he now?'

'No one knows. He hasn't been sighted—at least not in his costume—since the accident in the Walbridge Museum lecture hall. His true identity is a mystery because no one has ever seen his face under his mask. He may even be right here in this school without any of us knowing it.'

'Hmm.' Dickie looked down at the ground, nervously biting his fingernails. He wasn't quite sure what to say.

Penny leaned forward and placed a hand on his knee. 'I've told you all this, Dickie, because I like you.' She looked into his eyes and smiled a sad, gentle smile. 'I've enjoyed all our conversations over the last few months, and I've started to see you like a younger brother.'

Younger brother? But he didn't want to be a brother to her. He wanted to....

'You care about me, don't you,' continued Penny, interrupting his thoughts. 'I only realised that when you spoke to me after the dance. I like you caring for me, but, you see, I'm from another universe. I have different thoughts, different desires, and my home is somewhere else. There could never be anything romantic between us, but I hope we can still be friends.'

Dickie tried to hold back the tears. He was trembling. He tried to speak but he couldn't, and in the silence his thoughts told him lies.

'What she's really telling you is that she doesn't love you.

'You're not good enough for her, and you'll never be good enough.

'She's had enough of you pestering her all the time, and she's giving you the brush-off.'

Dickie timidly looked across at Penny. She was still smiling, and she looked just like the same wonderful Penny that Dickie knew (or thought he knew) so well. But she wasn't the Penny that he knew, was she? In fact, he had never known her at all. She was a poodle.

A poodle?

He was suddenly aware of Penny's hand on his knee. This wasn't a human who was touching him. It was a strange alien creature. He felt repulsed, and he jumped out of his seat.

'Y-you're a poodle,' he said as he slowly backed away from her. He looked scared and grief-stricken at the same time. 'Why can't you be Penny? That's who I want you to be.'

'But I am Penny,' she insisted, holding out her hand as a sign of friendship. 'It's just that you never knew before that I was....'

Penny didn't finish the sentence; Dickie was no longer in the room to hear her. He had run outside, confused and not wanting to hear any more, and he was going to run all the way home until he reached the warm security of his bedroom. He had some serious thinking to do.

Penny wept in the quietness of the tuck shop room. Things weren't going too well for her. She was trapped in a universe where she didn't belong. It looked highly unlikely that she would ever get back home. And now she was more alone than ever because she had frightened off a good friend at a time when she desperately needed friends.

In a brief moment of optimism she tried to convince herself that things would soon get better.

Maybe the 'Wow' Screen would soon be repaired. Maybe she and Jonathan would soon be able to return safely to their universe where they could forget that this long ordeal had ever happened. Maybe fortune would shine down upon them for once, in a world where there didn't seem to be too many happy endings.

Maybe poodles could fly.

Part Three

Oodles of Poodles

11

Dickie Dustbin looked sadly across the Heathlands School library at Penny Green. He was sitting near the back by the encyclopedias, and Penny was serving at the front desk, currently signing out a hardback copy of *Three Cheers, Secret Seven* for Mr Coombes, the school headmaster, who was an Enid Blyton fan.

Dickie had just been through the worst few days of his life. Since leaving Penny on Friday night, he had spent most of the weekend sulking in his bedroom, only coming down for the spy film on telly on Saturday and for the mid-day meal on Sunday. His mum took all his other meals up to him, and he didn't always eat them. His parents were very concerned.

'What's wrong with you, son?' his mum had asked him on Saturday after taking him a plate of bacon and cheese sandwiches and a bowl of freshly-cooked apple crumble with steaming hot custard. Dickie had uncharacteristically refused to eat them. 'You normally scoff three times as much food as you need, but today you've hardly eaten a thing.' (If he didn't have that superpower that allowed him to eat as much food as he wanted without gaining weight or feeling sick, he could have blamed his unusual lack of appetite on all the Mars bars he had speedily consumed at the school disco. But it wasn't the Mars bars that were affecting him.) 'Is there something bothering you?'

'No, Mum,' Dickie had lied, trying to reassure her, but not doing it very well because he had a glum expression on his face that was worrying her. 'I...I just don't feel hungry, that's all.'

His dad had gone up to see him a few times as well.

'What is it, Dickie?' he had asked, sitting on the bed beside him. 'I've never seen you so miserable. Have those bullies at school been upsetting you again?'

'No, Dad. It's just...it's probably just that I've been working too hard at school recently, that's all.'

His parents knew he wasn't telling the truth, especially his claim that he was suffering from overwork. That was the funniest thing his dad had heard all week. But they didn't force him into a confession. Maybe it was something he needed to work out for himself. And anyway, it would probably all be over by the time he was back with his friends at school on Monday.

But it was now Monday lunchtime, and Dickie was still down in the dumps.

Penny's unusual revelation on Friday night had thrown Dickie into a deep state of confusion. He was still in love with her...he thought. But he was now also angry with her for not being who he wanted her to be. Or maybe he was just angry at himself for his stupidity these last few months by being in love with her. He couldn't really tell. Either way, he knew now that he could never have a proper relationship with her. It would be wrong for him to have a girlfriend who was a dog.

Thump!

'Uh-oh!' thought Dickie.

The door of the school library had been kicked open by a particularly unpleasant fifth-former called 'Crusher' Craig. His proper name was Craig Biggs, but he was more commonly known as 'Crusher' because of his frequent bullying activities around the school. Marching as loudly as possible behind him were the five fellow fifth-formers who always followed him around. All of them were scared to death of him, but they tried to cover this up by acting as tough as possible and making life miserable for the pupils they picked on. Penny looked up at them and groaned, not because she was scared of them (they didn't intimidate her in the slightest), but because of all the trouble they caused when they came into the library, such as stealing books from the shelves or throwing things at people who were trying to study. For fifth-formers, Penny thought, they acted very immaturely. Why couldn't they grow up?

As they shuffled along the floor, coughing and loudly muttering among themselves, Penny said to them all: 'Excuse me, but could you possibly be a bit quieter in here, please.'

'What?' grunted Crusher, and the five behind him gasped in horror, terrified of what he might do. Apart from Penny and Crusher, there was now complete silence in the library. The atmosphere was tense, and all eyes had turned to the confrontation at the front.

'What was that you said?' Crusher was annoyed.

How dare anyone tell him off...especially a girl. He wasn't going to let her get away with this.

'I said, "Be quiet, please," ' repeated Penny, still managing to remain calm. 'There are people working in here, and you're all being very inconsiderate, thinking you can just barge in and make as much noise as you want.'

The gang-member next to Crusher began sniggering nervously, but Crusher kicked him in the shins, his way of telling him to stop. This was no laughing matter.

'Ow,' went the gang-member in pain.

Crusher advanced towards the front desk and looked straight down into Penny's eyes. Penny could now see right up his nose, and she could also smell his terrible bad breath.

'Listen, you. I'll make as much noise as I want, thank you very much,' Crusher fumed.

'That's fine by me,' persisted Penny, bravely smiling up at him. 'I like making noise myself on occasions, believe it or not. However, I must insist that you and your friends move to another location for all your noise-making, because this library is supposed to remain quiet.'

'Why, you....' Crusher pulled Penny up by her shoulders. He wasn't sure what he was going to do with her, but it was bound to be something violent.

'Get your hands off her, Craig!' shouted another fifth-former who had just entered the room. It was Jonathan Matthews, known by everyone in the school as Penny Green's boyfriend, and, in reality, another poodle from the poodle planet earth.

Crusher turned round.

'Who's that?' he said, and then he gulped. 'Oh, hello, Jonathan,' he said, suddenly looking timid.

'Just having a nice chat with your girlfriend here. Ha ha.' He let go of Penny's shoulders and let her sit back down again. Then he faced his gang, none of them quite sure whether to continue looking tough and menacing, or to act friendly towards Jonathan like their leader. 'Come on, lads,' Crusher urged them. 'I think maybe it's time we should leave. Let's have a smoke outside instead.'

As they quickly left—Crusher leaving more quickly than the rest, and also a lot more quietly than when he'd entered—Jonathan marched over to Penny.

'Are you okay?' he asked her, whispering because he didn't want to disturb anyone.

'Yes, fine,' she said, also whispering. 'Craig and that lot don't really bother me. They're all words and threats and nothing much else. Mind you, for a moment there I thought Craig really *was* going to hit me. Thanks for coming in at the right time.'

'That's okay,' said Jonathan. 'Ever since my confrontation with the so-called "Crusher" last term on the playing field he's been reluctant to clash with me again.'

'I know. And he deserved it, the brute, pushing you around like that and calling you all those names. It took ages for that black eye you gave him to disappear.'

Good for Penny, thought Dickie, who had been watching intently from the back ever since Crusher's dramatic entrance. Yes, he *did* still love her he now realised, especially after seeing her bravely stick up to Crusher like that; something he would never have been able to do himself. What a woman. What a poodle. Oh yes, that was right. She was a poodle, wasn't she? He kept forgetting.

'Anyway, the reason I came here,' revealed Jonathan, 'was to tell you that Professor Boggles wants to see us after the school assembly this afternoon.'

'Professor Boggles?'

'Yes. Mr Ryfield just told me. He's visiting the school today, and after he's spoken at the afternoon assembly he wants to have a few words with us, presumably about his "Wow" Screen that he's rebuilding to try and get us home.' Jonathan was still whispering, this time not because he didn't want to disturb the others in the library, but because he didn't want anyone to hear all of his and Penny's secrets. 'When we saw him at his house two weeks ago he said he'd almost finished.'

Penny didn't look too hopeful.

'I do hope he *has* finished,' she said, but she pessimistically added: 'I wouldn't count on it, though. The professor's been promising us things for over a year now, and we're still stuck in the human being universe.'

'But maybe this is it now,' said Jonathan. He seemed to be saying it more to convince himself than Penny. 'Maybe we *are* now going home.'

'Yes, maybe.' Penny smiled, and she affectionately squeezed Jonathan's hand. 'Maybe.'

Dickie looked down at the masterpiece he'd just been working on. He'd come into the library to revise for Wednesday's history test, but, as usual, he'd got sidetracked. Now before him was a detailed portrait of Mr Hobbs, his Religious Education teacher, complete with a dark Dracula-type cape, and sharp fangs sticking out of his mouth with blood dripping off them.

Dickie didn't like Mr Hobbs at all, and neither did

most of the other pupils at Heathlands. He was always grumpy during his lessons, and he always seemed to be telling pupils off, even the hard-working ones. No one was excluded from the wrath of Mr Hobbs. Dickie didn't know what his problem was. He'd been teaching for a long time now (he was very close to retirement age), so maybe he was just fed up with his job. He was certainly very bitter. If Mr Hobbs represented what religion was all about, Dickie didn't want anything to do with it.

Dickie thought his picture was so good that he decided to make a photocopy of it. He was going to keep the copy himself, and send the original to *Ghastly Ghoulies*, a weekly horror comic that he read. They sometimes printed readers' drawings on the letters page.

He dug deep into his pockets to see if he had 10p for the library's photocopying machine. Yes, he had more than enough: *two* ten pence pieces. He strolled over to the machine and placed his drawing face-down on the glass, dropping one of the 10ps in the coin slot and pushing the 'Print' button. Seconds later, an exact copy of the vampire Mr Hobbs slid out of the left-hand side of the machine. Dickie picked it up and smiled. It was almost as good as the original.

He still had 10p left. An idea came to him, and he looked around. Penny was still talking to Jonathan so she wouldn't notice. And the others in the library were busy studying (for a change). He would have to be quick. Dickie had wanted to do this for ages. He didn't know why. Some strange inner compulsion was driving him. Maybe it was a waste of 10p, but it was something he just had to do.

He dropped his second 10p in the slot, and quickly pressed his face on the glass. Then he shut his eyes as tight as he could and pushed the 'Print' button. As soon as the light inside had scanned across his features, a sheet of paper came out of the left-hand side of the machine that was grey and grainy, but still contained a recognisable likeness of his face.

Dickie quietly laughed when he examined this, and then he returned to his seat at the back of the library so that he could put all his stuff back inside his bag. The bell for the end of lunch would be ringing soon, and everyone would have to go to the main hall for the afternoon assembly.

When Jonathan left the library he saw the school caretaker with a lisp talking to 'Crusher' Craig and his gang. It sounded like he was inviting Craig and co to a party at his place that evening.

Jonathan didn't think much about this. Why should he? He had more important things on his mind, such as what Professor Alfred Boggles would be saying to him and Penny after the assembly.

12

The pupils sat transfixed in the Heathlands School main hall, with a quietness that was rare. Normally they'd keep fidgeting and muttering among themselves during assemblies, and some of them even had burping contests, seeing who could burp the loudest without being told off. The reason for everyone's unusual attentiveness today was the talk by

Professor Alfred Boggles. At first all the pupils had sniggered, making fun of his strange accent and eccentric appearance. (Professor Boggles looked just as eccentric in his human form as he did as a poodle.) But as he continued talking they all became fascinated with what he was saying.

He was talking about a new chemical he'd been working on that brought dead plants 'back to life', and he demonstrated its life-giving properties by pouring a few drops from a glass beaker onto a wilted daffodil in a vase. To the amazement of all the teachers and pupils, the daffodil quickly perked up before their very eyes, standing upright and bright yellow again as if it was freshly picked. The professor went on to explain that he'd also tried the chemical on dead rats and insects, but so far he hadn't succeeded on anything other than plants. If, however, he could somehow make the chemical stronger or find a vital new ingredient to make it work on non-plant life, the implications were staggering. What if, for instance, it could be used on human beings?

When the assembly had finished, there was a rush of teachers and pupils to the front to talk to the professor. Crusher Craig was standing behind Dickie in the crowd, and he was up to no good as usual.

'Here, stop pulling my hair!' protested Dickie, and he angrily turned round to see who was treating him this way.

'Oops,' he went when he saw that it was Crusher, and he feebly mumbled: 'Ha ha. Sorry about that, Crusher. I...erm...thought you were someone else. You can pull my hair as much as you like.'

Crusher looked furious, and he obviously wasn't satisfied with Dickie's apology.

'That's not good enough, Dustbin,' Crusher

fumed. 'You told me to stop pulling your hair, and no one *ever* talks to me like that!'

'Gulp!' thought Dickie.

He said it as well.

'Gulp,' said Dickie.

Then Dickie went 'Oof!' as Crusher pushed him backwards, and he soon went 'Oof!' again as his head painfully made contact with the table on which the professor had put all his scientific equipment. The beaker containing the professor's precious liquid—which had been resting near the edge of the table top—fell over the side. Luckily the beaker didn't land on Dickie, who was now moaning on the ground, and it didn't smash into a thousand pieces on the floor either. Instead, it landed inside Dickie's school bag.

Immediately there was a fizzing sound, and smoke rose from inside.

Professor Boggles was horrified.

'Hey! Votch out!' he screamed. 'Dat stuff iss dangerous!' He reached into Dickie's bag and carefully extracted the beaker. Luckily not too much liquid had been lost.

He glared disapprovingly at Crusher as he placed the beaker back on the table.

'You stupidt boy,' he said. 'Dat stuff iss like acid. You could haff really hurt somevon.' He was obviously very angry.

'Aye yi yi,' mumbled the professor, something he mumbled whenever he was annoyed. People then whispered things like, ' "Aye yi yi"? What on earth does that mean?', and, 'No wonder he's known as a loony professor if he says things like that.'

A voice of authority in the crowd soon interrupted the whispers.

'Don't worry, Professor,' it said. 'I'll take care of this troublemaker for you.' The voice belonged to Mr Ryfield, the deputy headmaster. He took Crusher by the scruff of the neck, and said: 'I've had enough of your bullying. It's straight to the headmaster for you. Something's going to be done about you once and for all.'

'Ulp,' went Crusher, who was even more scared of Mr Ryfield than he was of Jonathan Matthews. For all of his apparent toughness, Crusher was a coward at heart.

Dickie slowly got up from the floor and faced the professor. His head was throbbing and he didn't look too good.

'Sorry about that,' he apologised nervously, in awe of this great man of science. 'I didn't mean to....'

'No need to apolochise,' said Professor Boggles. 'I saw everythink. It vossn't your fault. It voss dat awful bully. I'm chust glad you're not hurt.'

As Dickie bent down to pick up his bag, Professor Boggles made an announcement to the crowd.

'Sorry chaps and chapesses,' he said, 'but I can't answer any more kvestions. It's time for me to pack avay. I don't vont any more accidents to happen.'

There was some grumbling at this, but most people cheerfully complied with the professor's wishes and made their way out of the school hall. Most people, that is, except for Jonathan and Penny.

When everyone else had left the hall and no one could hear them, Jonathan asked the professor: 'So how are things going with the "Wow" Screen?'

The professor didn't look at them when he answered this, and he seemed quite uncomfortable. That was because he had something very difficult to tell them.

'Der screen vill be ready diss veek,' he promised while packing away his equipment, 'but....'

'But what, Professor?' Penny was concerned. 'What's wrong?'

For the first time that day Professor Boggles looked directly across at both of them, instead of at his equipment or down at the ground. What he had to say was obviously very serious.

(Warning to the reader: there will now follow a lengthy and moderately dull speech from the professor. If, like most people, you find his dialect almost incomprehensible, you have my full permission to do something more profitable the next few minutes, like maybe feeding your budgie or making a mug of hot Horlicks. Then, when he's finished rabbitting on, I'll give you a brief summary of what he said—in *proper* English.)

'I must stress to you both der enormous risk you'll be takink if you go through vith diss,' the professor solemnly informed them. 'Der screen's goink to be able to do vot it voss originally designed to do: look at beinks from udder universes. But ass for transportink people from von universe to anudder....' He resumed the packing away of his equipment. 'Vot happened a year ago voss a freak accident. If we try undt duplicate der circumstances, who knows vot might happen? You could end up in your universe, I suppose, but vot if it dussn't vork? We are dealink with thinks here vitch ve don't completely understandt. You could both get hurt...or even die.'

(Now for the promised brief summary: the professor doesn't know if his newly-reconstructed 'Wow' Screen is going to get Jonathan and Penny back to their universe, and they may die very

100

horribly if they decide to go ahead with jumping into the screen. Cor, isn't this exciting!)

Jonathan and Penny didn't say a word. There was nothing much they *could* say really.

'Anyvay,' continued the professor, 'dat iss basically vot I vonted to tell you both. Der "Vow" Screen should be ready on Friday, but I can't promise success, and I vonted you to be avare off vot you could be lettink yourselfs in for.'

His packing finished, he plonked his small case on the floor and concluded: 'So, do you both vont to come round to my house on Friday eveninik to try undt get back to your universe?'

It was a hard decision—possibly the toughest decision that Jonathan and Penny would *ever* have to make. They had known all along that a repeat trip through the 'Wow' Screen may not be successful, but they'd never realised before just how dangerous that repeat trip might be...and they may even have to pay with their lives. Both of them felt sick. What on earth should they do?

Before they had a chance to answer, a large kangaroo came leaping into the school hall and bounced over to Professor Boggles. On closer inspection, the professor realised that this wasn't a real kangaroo at all but someone dressed up as one. There was a colourful party hat on its head, pink flippers on its feet, and it was blowing one of those clever whistles you can buy at toy shops that makes slightly rude noises.

'Good afternoon, sir,' the kangaroo announced in a phony deep voice, as it continued to bounce up and down. 'I am a kanga-gram, and I—puff—have come to wish you an exceedingly happy birthday.'

The professor, along with Penny and Jonathan,

watched in astonishment as the kanga-gram proceeded to sing a song in honour of Professor Boggles' birthday. The professor was even more astonished than the others because he knew that his birthday wouldn't be for another five months.

It was hard to make out some of the words at times, because the kanga-gram jumped up and down while it sang, and it was often out of breath. However, exclusively within these pages, I am now allowed to reveal to you all the words of the song:

Happy Birthday, Mr. Boggles
Copyright © Some twit in a kangaroo suit 1990

Happy birthday, Mr. Boggles.
Here's a song to wish you well.
I admire your daft inventions.
You're okay. I think you're swell.

Chorus:

>Hope you have a happy birthday.
>Tum ti tum, beef stroganoff.
>La la la la la la la la.
>You're all right, you clever prof.

This kanga-gram is sent to you
By someone who's your closest mate.
He sent it to commemorate
The fact that you've turned sixty-eight.

Chorus:

>Hope you have a happy birthday.
>Tum ti tum, beef stroganoff.
>La la la la la la la la.
>You're all right, you clever prof.

Dramatic ending (sung slowly but very loudly):

You're all right, you clever prof.

Professor Boggles didn't like the last verse of the song where it said that he was sixty-eight years old. How dare anyone say that he was that old. He was only sixty-five.

He was just about to voice his objection to this when the kanga-gram fished a small parcel from its artificial pouch. It handed the parcel to the professor, and the professor's mood suddenly went from extreme annoyance to pleasant surprise.

'Thank you very much,' he said, eagerly snatching the parcel. 'I vonder vot could be in here.'

He slowly disposed of the wrapping paper in a scientific and methodical way (peeling off the sticky tape and carefully unfolding the paper), and found inside twenty packets of Trebor Refreshers and a medium-sized tee-shirt with a picture on it of Albert Einstein sticking his tongue out.

'Einstein! Mein hero!' exclaimed Professor Boggles, delighted with his presents. 'Undt Refreshers ass vell! I love dem!' The professor handed a packet each to Penny and Jonathan. 'Here, haff some vunderful Refreshers!'

They both took their packet, but they didn't look very grateful. In fact, they both seemed downright gloomy.

Professor Boggles was a very observant person, even though he was a loony professor, and he noticed their gloominess instantly.

'Vot iss vrong with you two?' he asked. 'Iss it to do vith Friday night?'

Jonathan glanced at Penny, then answered for both of them.

'Can we give you our decision tomorrow?' he requested. 'I think Penny and I need to do some serious talking about whether we should go ahead with this.'

'I understandt,' said the professor, and he waved goodbye as they walked hand-in-hand out of the school hall. Both of them looked as if they had just seen a ghost, and there wasn't the usual bounce in their steps as they walked. Instead, it looked as if they were taking part in a funeral march.

The school bell rang once they'd left the hall, and all the pupils at Heathlands disappeared into their classrooms for the next lesson of the day.

Dickie Dustbin gulped as he walked into the Religious Education class; he wasn't looking forward to the lesson at all. Dickie's RE teacher, Mr Hobbs, gave him the creeps, and somehow he just knew that Mr Hobbs was going to pick on him this lesson.

13

Professor Boggles, still in the school hall, turned to the kanga-gram and said: 'Thank you Mr Kanga-Gram for der song undt der kind pressents, but I'm afraid it issn't my birthday for a long time yet.'

'Isn't it?' The kanga-gram stopped bouncing up and down; it was obviously disappointed. 'Crumbs. I must have got the dates mixed up in my diary. How embarrassing.'

The professor looked suspiciously at the kanga-gram.

'Who exactly are you?' he asked. 'Do I know you from somevere?'

The kanga-gram flung out its arms and demanded: 'Guess!'

'Hmm.' The professor was deep in thought. 'Are you Sydney Balloons, der retired ferret breeder who lives down der road?' was his first guess.

'Nope,' answered the kanga-gram.

'How about Alexander Goalposts, dat nice man in der greengrocers who vunce played 'Der Floral Dance' vith hiss armpits for Esther Rantzen's *Dat's Life*?'

'Wrong. Try again.'

'Erm....'

There was silence for a few moments, then inspiration struck the professor.

'I know who you are!' he declared. He was joyful because he knew he was right. 'Only von person I know would be so crazy ass to dress up ass a kangaroo for mein birthday—undt *den* get der dates mixed up. You're Charlie Digestives, aren't you!'

'Well done!' Charlie took the kangaroo head off his own head to reveal his true, world-famous features. He was smiling. 'Sorry about getting my dates mixed up, Professor,' he apologised, using his proper voice. 'I was in a rush when I looked in my diary this morning, and I could have sworn it said that it was *your* birthday. It *does* say in there that it's someone's birthday today. I wonder whose it could be?'

He rubbed his sweaty forehead with the kangaroo head (it was hot in that costume), and continued, 'Anyway, while I'm here, Professor, I couldn't possibly ask you a favour, could I?'

'Try me.'

'Well....' Charlie nervously stared down at his flippers. He was about to bare his soul, and he felt quite awkward because he wasn't used to doing that. 'Recently I've been thinking about things, you see.'

'Vot sort off thinks?'

'You know, the meaning of everything. Why we're all here. God and that.'

'Are you gettink relichious, Charlie?'

'Religious? Me? No...I mean, yes...I think.... Oh, I don't know.' He scraped the flippers backwards and forwards on the dusty wooden floorboards. 'I've never told anyone this before, but about a year ago— the same time as the 'Wow' Screen catastrophe—two strange things happened to me. They've been bothering me since then—I haven't been able to get them out of my mind—and they've made me think a lot about stuff that I never used to consider important.'

'So how can I help?'

Charlie looked directly across at his colleague. 'I'd appreciate a chat with you sometime. You're a man of science, Professor. You deal with things like the universe and creation and stuff. Maybe you could answer some of my questions.'

Professor Boggles was flattered that Charlie thought he could help. 'I don't know about dat, mein friend,' he modestly admitted, 'but I can certainly try, I suppose. I'm free tonight if you vont me to come round.'

'Excellent!' said Charlie.

'Vill half-seven be all right?'

'Half-seven's fine. I'll make sure Ethel has the usual Tizer and Twiglets out for you.'

'Splendiferoso.'

Charlie looked down at his watch on the wrist of

his costume. 'Whoops, is that the time? I must get going.' He put the kangaroo head back on. 'I've a busy afternoon ahead of me,' he explained. 'First I've got to return this costume to the fancy dress shop; then I need to capture the Dastardly Doughnut-Eater from Dagenham, the Pesky Pilchard Pilferer from Putney, and the Raving Rice Pudding from Richmond—and all before *Neighbours* on the telly at half-past five.'

'It's a tough life beink a world-famous detective.'

'Too true. See you tonight, Prof, and thanks for agreeing to help.'

'Righto.' Professor Boggles waved goodbye as Charlie happily bounced away—and then he jumped with shock when he felt an unexpected hand on his shoulder.

The professor hadn't jumped for a long time. 'Whee!' he went in mid-air, and he jumped a few more times because he realised he quite liked it. Then he turned to see who the hand belonged to.

'Ah, hello Misster Ryfieldt. How very goodt to see you again.'

'Thank you, Professor,' said Mr Ryfield. 'I just wanted to apologise for the disturbance caused by that difficult pupil; he's been dealt with appropriately, I can assure you. Thank you also for taking the assembly today. It was most enlightening.'

'Not at—puff—all,' wheezed the professor, jumping up and down again and thoroughly enjoying himself. His long flowing beard hit him on his forehead every time he landed on the ground. 'It voss—gassp—mein pleasure.'

Someone who *wasn't* thoroughly enjoying himself was Dickie Dustbin, seated near the back of the Religious Education class.

'In this common-sense, scientific age,' droned Mr Hobbs, 'why do people persist in believing that you can know God personally, like a friend? God is much too big to want to be involved with people like us. And as for all the so-called miracles in the Bible, I'm sure they can be explained as perfectly natural occurrences. The essence of religion to me is simply being the best person you can possibly be. That's all there is to it. Miracles? Knowing God? Pah! Rubbish!'

Dickie's mind wasn't on what Mr Hobbs was saying. For someone who claimed to know everything about God and religion, Mr Hobbs seemed the most miserable man on earth. It didn't look as if his beliefs had helped him very much. No, Dickie had too many other things on his mind. For a start he was still confused about his feelings towards Penny Green, and he also found it hard to accept her claims that there were lots of other worlds like earth in other universes. It was overwhelming just trying to think about it.

But the main thing on Dickie's mind was his terrible throbbing headache which he got from his fall to the ground after Professor Boggles' assembly. He also felt an intense hatred for Crusher Craig. Previously he had only been afraid of Craig; he didn't hate him. But his humiliation after the assembly had been the final straw, and Dickie tried to think up different ways to get his own back, many of them much too violent for me to write down here.

Mr Hobbs noticed that Dickie's mind was elsewhere, and he demanded: 'So what do you think about that, Master Dustbin?'

'Hmm. Huh...what?'

A tense silence filled the classroom. Everyone knew that Mr Hobbs was easily angered, and

Dickie's 'Hmm. Huh...what?'—as trivial and insignificant as it may seem to you—was almost sure to provoke the teacher's terrible wrath.

'What was that, boy?'

Dickie was suddenly horribly aware that every eye in the classroom was staring straight at him, including the penetrating glare of the seething Mr Hobbs. He didn't know how to answer since he hadn't heard a word of what Hobbs had been waffling on about. But he tried to say something anyway so that he wouldn't look stupid.

'I...' he began, which unfortunately had the opposite effect. His hesitation and obvious uncertainty proved to the class his ignorance of what had been said in the lesson so far.

'I...' he continued, perspiration breaking out on his forehead (which is often what happens when you get nervous). He felt terribly self-conscious, and he hated being the centre of attention.

After his third 'I...' something quite remarkable happened. So intense was it in its wonderfulness that it nearly blew Dickie away; so stunned was he by it that it took him a while to catch his breath. He didn't notice that something had started moving in his school bag.

Light...everywhere there was light. The classroom, which previously seemed dull and drab, was alive with bright, cheerful colours which surrounded and engulfed Dickie. It was as if Dickie had been blind all his life and was seeing for the first time. It was as if he had always had a black-and-white television set, and for the first time ever was seeing programmes in colour. The universe was alive, exciting and a glorious place to be in.

Everything made sense. The grass and the trees

outside. The desks inside, and all the books on the bookshelves and the paintings on the wall. Even the dust and the insects on the floor. Everything was there for a purpose...for a reason. It was just...right. *Everything was there for a reason!*

Dickie felt good about everyone and everything. He no longer hated Crusher Craig. In fact, he felt rather sorry for him. And as for how he felt about Penny...wow! Words just couldn't describe it.

Dickie looked strangely serene, and there was an unmistakable glow on his face.

Without thinking, he looked up and said: 'I love you, Mr Hobbs.'

All of Dickie's classmates immediately burst into laughter, but Mr Hobbs didn't seem the slightest bit amused. In fact he was rather annoyed because he presumed (understandably) that Dickie was taking the mickey.

Dickie, not embarrassed in the slightest, wondered why everyone was laughing. He had really meant what he said.

'What was that, boy?' Mr Hobbs' nostrils were flaring, and his cheeks were red with rage.

'I said I...'

Before Dickie could finish, another voice—which sounded exactly the same as Dickie's—interrupted him.

'I hate you, Mr Hobbs,' snarled the muffled voice. 'You're nothing but a stupid old man who never achieved anything important in his life. No one likes you, your lessons are boring, and I hate you, hate you, hate you!'

The giggling stopped, and silence reigned in the room.

Dickie was in deep trouble. After all, wasn't it *his*

voice that had spoken? Everyone knew that something awful was going to happen, and the dangerous atmosphere in the room was unbearable. Some pupils nervously looked out of the window, not looking forward to what was going to happen next. Others pretended to be engrossed in their RE text books, or bent down to tie up their shoelaces. None of them wanted to catch the gaze of Mr Hobbs in case he took his anger out on them.

Dickie, still serene, didn't know where the voice had come from, but as far as Mr Hobbs was concerned it was Dickie who had insulted him so cruelly.

The change in Mr Hobbs' face over the next few seconds was fascinating. It started off red, then rapidly went through every colour of the rainbow towards blue, as he got steadily angrier and angrier. His ears pulsated in a frenzy of fury, his eyebrows fluttered like excited caterpillars, and his lips trembled as the words of bitterness that were forming inside his mouth tried to escape prematurely.

Eventually he boomed: 'Dustbin, you've gone too far! You've gone....'

Silence. Mr Hobbs was unusually quiet. No one had *ever* heard Mr Hobbs stop shouting in midsentence before.

A tear came to his eye, but no one got the chance to see it. Mr Hobbs didn't want any of his pupils to notice that he was upset, so he stormed out of the room as fast as he could, loudly slamming the door behind him to show that he was still angry. He didn't return for the rest of the lesson.

Dickie Dustbin was suddenly the hero of the class. Everyone hated Mr Hobbs, and Dickie was the one who had finally made him speechless. For the rest of the lesson people kept going over to his desk to congratulate him. Some sang songs in his honour, and others gave him sweets and leftover bits of packed lunch to show their appreciation.

Dickie wasn't sure that he liked everyone's adulation, especially when it was for something as despicable as insulting a fellow human being, no matter how unlovely that human being was. He didn't know where all those nasty words came from that sounded like him, and he also didn't understand why he suddenly felt so good about things—even about Mr Hobbs. Dickie, because of his confusion, remained relatively quiet and thoughtful, while the others in the class laughed and joked and generally made the most of their unexpected freedom.

Mr Hobbs, now outside, determinedly marched towards his car and passed the school caretaker in the staff car park.

'Afternoon, Mr Hobbth,' said the caretaker, raking up dead leaves from the concrete. 'What are you doing out tho early? Don't you normally teach a clath at thith time?'

Mr Hobbs didn't want the caretaker to see that he was despondent, so he went all grumpy again.

'None of your business!' he snapped, reaching his vehicle and sliding his key in the lock. 'I've taught at this school for more than thirty years, so I can jolly well do whatever I want with my time!'

'Perfect. Just perfect,' thought the caretaker. 'This is just the sort of person I want at my house tonight.' (As you can see, the caretaker didn't think with a lisp—he only spoke with one.)

He took a photocopied invitation from his coat pocket, and handed it to the miserable Religious Education teacher.

'Do you want to come to a party tonight?' he asked. 'It'th going to be at my houth. A few friendth will be coming round, and we're going to....'

At that moment a detective in a kangaroo suit bounced across the car park to get to his Ford Escort. The detective, of course, was Charlie Digestives, and he stopped when he heard the school caretaker inviting Mr Hobbs to his party.

'Just a minute,' he thought. 'I've heard that voice somewhere before. That's....'

There was a moment's hesitation. 'No. It can't be,' Charlie eventually said, sounding disappointed. 'He didn't have a lisp, did he? Pity. I've been after him for ages.'

Then inspiration struck him. 'The birthday! It's not Professor Boggles' birthday at all, is it? It's *my* birthday. Of course it is. Mine! And I'm thirty-three! Yippee!'

Charlie was so pleased about it being his birthday that he sang 'Tie Me Kangaroo Down, Sport' while he bounced the final few yards to his car. Never let it be said that Charlie Digestives didn't appreciate good music.

14

Dickie Dustbin's last lesson of the day was Geography. It was pretty uninspiring—mostly about market gardening in the north of England and other stuff like that. He spent most of the lesson staring out of the window, watching grey squirrels playfully skipping around, foraging for acorns. He also enjoyed listening to the birds happily twittering and a calm wind softly blowing through the leaves of the trees. Wonderful. Simply wonderful. Dickie had always enjoyed nature and the countryside and things like that, but for some reason everything seemed so much better today. He wasn't just seeing and hearing these things. In some strange, unexplainable way he was also feeling them—experiencing them. He knew exactly why everything outside was the way it was…and everything was *just right*.

Except for humans. It was funny. Dickie was fond of his classmates—and even his teachers—in a way that he had never been before. But he was also more aware of all their faults and weaknesses—painfully aware of them. He could sense the darkness that was in the people around him: all the potential for doing bad things; all the hate and bitterness that people kept stored up inside; and all the rotten thoughts that they had about each other. Dickie found it hard to cope with some of the strong emotions that came with his new awareness. He tried to block them out by looking at the playful innocence of the squirrels again.

Soon the bell for the end of school rang. Dickie

sighed contentedly, cracking his knuckles because he was happy in a deeper way than usual, then leisurely walked out of the Geography room with his school bag in his hand. His bag was heavier than usual for some reason, but Dickie didn't notice because he was too wrapped up in all the wonderful new things he was experiencing.

Dickie strolled out through the school gates in a blissful daze, oblivious to all the people saying 'Goodbye' or 'Well done' as they ran past, or patting him on the back because of what he had said to Mr Hobbs. Obviously the news of his supposed boldness in RE this afternoon had spread throughout the school, and Dickie was a hero.

Derek Jones, a tubby lad from the third year, offered Dickie a tube of Smarties and a week-old stick of liquorice that he had only half chewed. Dickie walked straight past him, not acknowledging his presence in the slightest.

Katrina Barclay, a delightfully bubbly blonde from the fourth year, gave him a long wet kiss on the cheek because she admired what he had done. Dickie didn't even notice that she was there. (It was strange Dickie not noticing a kiss.)

In the woods on a short cut to home, Dickie's blissful daze was interrupted by a voice from inside his school bag. It was the voice that had hurled all those nasty insults at Mr Hobbs—the one that had sounded like Dickie's, only muffled and uncharacteristically hateful.

'Oy, get me out of here!'

'Hmm? What?' Dickie stopped; the interruption had startled him into full attentiveness. 'Did I hear someone shouting?'

Because the voice was muffled, Dickie assumed

that it came from somewhere in the distance. But no matter where he looked—squinting to block out the distracting rays of the sun—he couldn't see anyone.

He shrugged his shoulders and carried on walking.

'Didn't you hear me, mush? Get me out of this thing!'

Dickie stopped again. The voice sounded as if it came from inside his school bag. But how?

Dickie put the bag down on the ground and slowly unzipped it. Immediately, out popped the photocopy that Dickie had made of his face. It made a thump as it hit the ground (it was much heavier than a normal sheet of paper), and the face on the photocopy looked strangely three-dimensional.

'About time!' the photocopy snapped at Dickie, its grainy black-and-white lips moving in time with what it said. 'I was bloomin' suffocating in there.'

'You—you're talking!'

'Well done, Dick! You're not as stupid as you look—and believe me, you look *very* stupid.' The photocopy bounced along the ground, thumping again as it did so. 'Grunt! I feel trapped in this paper,' it wheezed. 'Not enough room to move. I'm going to have to pop out.'

And it did just that. With much groaning and straining, the face eventually emerged from the paper, then shoulders, arms, legs, and finally two grubby shoes, identical (except in colour) to the ones that Dickie was wearing. The sheet of paper was now completely white, and it blew away in the wind; while a black-and-white version of Dickie stood proud and erect, his hands on his hips. The real Dickie was naturally astonished.

'How did you do that?' he gasped, not believing his eyes. 'What's going on?'

The photocopy snorted in contempt.

'I take it back,' he snarled. 'You *are* stupid. And to think I used to be part of you and all your goody-goody ideals. Pyeuh! It makes me feel sick!' The photocopy was spitting out his words. 'But that's all over now. I'm free from you, and I can do whatever I want.'

'Uh?' went Dickie, finding this hard to take in. Did he say that he used to be part of Dickie? What on earth was the photocopy talking about?

The photocopy, surveying the land around him— land that he could now freely move about in without Dickie's good side limiting him—loudly announced: 'And the first thing I'm going to do with my new freedom is have a good snog with Penny Green.' He smugly inhaled the cool outside air through his nostrils. 'Yes, I've wanted to get all intimate with that bird for months.'

'Penny?' Dickie was horrified. He loved Penny deeper now than he had ever done before, and he didn't want her to come to any harm from this sick, evil version of himself. 'No, don't!' he pleaded. 'I....'

Biff!

Dickie lay unconscious on the ground; the photocopy had just socked him one in the mush (that is to say, punched him in the face). Like Dickie, the photocopy wasn't particularly strong, but there was so much hate in his punch that it sent Dickie flying.

'Good. Now I'm rid of that creep.'

Smiling at a job well done, the photocopy made sure that no one was looking, then quickly stripped Dickie of his jumper, shirt, tie, trousers and shoes, so that all he had on was his underwear and socks. The

117

photocopy quickly put these colour clothes on over his black-and-white ones (how could Penny possibly think he was the real Dickie if he was totally black-and-white?), then ran in the general direction of Penny Green's house. And while running, he laughed a hideous evil laugh that all hideous evil baddies do in corny adventure books (unlike *this* book, which is absolutely brilliant and only slightly corny).

The next person on the short cut through the woods was Jonathan Matthews, happily singing the *Neighbours* theme.

'Neighbours. Everybody needs good....'

Suddenly he froze in his tracks because he saw Dickie on the ground. At first he thought that Dickie was dead, and a chill of horror went through him. But then he saw Dickie breathing, and, like the Good Samaritan in the Bible, he knelt down beside him to try to help.

'Dickie, Dickie,' he pleaded softly in his ear. 'Wake up. What's been going on?'

Nothing.

'Dickie, come on!' Jonathan urged, shouting this time and shaking him by the shoulders. 'What happened, for heaven's sake?'

There were a few moans and groans, then Dickie slowly opened his eyes.

'Uh...' was all he managed to say.

While Dickie recovered, Jonathan dressed him with the PE kit from his sports bag. Jonathan's kit was too big for Dickie—especially the trainers—but at least it covered up his semi-nakedness.

He then knelt beside Dickie again and asked him what had happened.

'Penny...in danger,' Dickie feebly answered.

Jonathan could barely hear him. 'He...the thing...it punched me...gone to see Penny.'

The thing? What did Dickie mean by 'the thing'?

Why did this thing take Dickie's school uniform?

And what was that Dickie had started off with? Oh yes, Penny was in danger.

'Penny's in danger?' Jonathan jumped up, obviously alarmed. 'This thing; did you say it's gone to Penny's house?'

'I think so,' whispered Dickie. He closed his eyes again. 'Ow, my head,' he complained. 'It's throbbing worse than ever.'

Jonathan needed to think quickly. Penny was in danger, and he had to do something. With a strong sense of urgency, he carried Dickie to a soft patch of grass away from the public footpath, and explained: 'Listen, Dickie, I'm just going to run over to Penny's place to see if she's all right. Then I'll come back for you, okay?'

'Okay,' Dickie agreed, between groans. 'But hurry, will you...please?'

'I promise.'

With all the determination of an Olympic runner, Jonathan sprinted through the woods, down a few side roads, then over to 23 Lindfield Avenue where Penny lived. He stood breathless outside the house, and barely had enough energy to ring the front door-bell.

The door was answered by Penny's mum.

'Hello, Jonathan,' she said, smiling because she liked Jonathan a lot. 'What can I do for you?'

'I—er—phew,' started Jonathan, still trying to regain his breath. 'I wanted—puff—to see how Penny's doing.'

'Penny? No, she hasn't come home yet.'

'She hasn't?'

'Well, she did...sort of.'

'Sort of?'

'Yes. I saw her through the front window. She was about to come down the garden path when that Dickie Dustbin boy ran over to her. I don't know what he said to her, but the next thing I knew they were walking down the road together.'

'Dickie Dustbin?' thought Jonathan. He screwed up his face while trying to figure this out. 'How odd. I was just with him in the woods.'

Penny's mum could see that he was troubled. 'What's wrong, Jonathan?' she asked, concerned at his puzzled expression.

Jonathan didn't answer her. Instead he enquired: 'Where do you reckon they went?'

'I'm not sure. But that's the direction they were headed in.' She pointed down the road.

Nothing from Jonathan for a few seconds.

'There *is* something wrong, isn't there?' Penny's mum persisted. 'What is it?'

'Penny's in danger.'

'What?'

'That's right. From Dickie.'

'Dickie Dustbin? Nonsense. He's one of the sweetest kids I know.'

More silence. Jonathan was obviously thinking.

'No, that wasn't Dickie she was with,' he soon deduced out loud.

'Not Dickie? But I saw him. He was....'

'...an imposter dressed up to look like him,' Jonathan finished for her.

'How do you know?'

'Because I was just with the *real* Dickie Dustbin in the woods back there. Someone beat him up and

120

stole most of his clothes, and that person—probably pretending to be Dickie—is now with Penny somewhere.'

Penny's mum wasn't entirely convinced about this Dickie look-alike theory—it all seemed a bit far-fetched—but she was naturally worried about her daughter.

'My goodness,' she said. 'If you're right we'd better do something quick.' She snatched the receiver from the hallway phone and frantically began dialling. 'Thanks for telling me all this, Jonathan. I'm going to call the police immediately.'

'And *I'm* going to get Dickie from the woods,' announced Jonathan. He ran back up the garden path. 'I won't be long,' he shouted.

All sorts of troubling questions went through Jonathan's mind as he sprinted back through the woods. First of all, Penny's mum was convinced that the person she saw Penny with was Dickie. This person must be an imposter, but how could he be so convincing? Secondly, Dickie referred to the person who beat him up as 'the thing'. Why did he call him 'the thing'? And finally, why was this 'thing' so interested in Penny?

All of Jonathan's questions—and more—would be answered by the time this fateful evening was through.

15

Allow me to go back in time about ten minutes. Penny Green is nearing her parents' house on Lindfield Avenue, and running up to her is the photocopy of Dickie Dustbin wearing most of Dickie's school clothes.

'Penny!' the photocopy yelled. 'Stop, please! I need to talk to you!'

'Dickie?' Penny turned round. 'What do you...Dickie, what's wrong? You look pale.'

'Pale? Oh, I guess I've caught the flu bug that's going round school. Listen'—the photocopy tried to sound polite like Dickie—'it's about today, right. I've been avoiding you at school...'

'Yes, I noticed.'

'...basically because I haven't known what to say to you. I'm still confused about what you told me on Friday night. Could we go somewhere, please, and have another chat?'

'Of course.'

'In private, please? By the river just off Brodrick Road?'

'Why not where I live?' She gestured towards her home. 'I can get you some coffee and biscuits.'

'Please,' the photocopy insisted, staring pleadingly into Penny's eyes. 'I'd rather talk by the river.'

'Hmm.' Penny stared back at the photocopy, hoping that maybe a close inspection of his features would reveal why she felt so uneasy. Dickie was his usual harmless self just now, polite and inoffensive. But underneath his niceness she could sense something not so nice. Why did Dickie seem so different? Penny could not put her finger on it.

'Okay, the river it is,' she soon gave in. 'I trust you.' But in her mind she added: 'At least, I *think* I trust you.'

The photocopy smiled, and that smile gave Penny the creeps. Instead of it being sweet and genuinely thankful, it communicated evil and unpleasant things to come. It was the sort of smile a nasty villain in a film would smile before he did whatever it is that nasty villains do.

Penny gasped, and the photocopy realised from her worried expression that he was slipping back into his normal wicked self and wasn't impersonating the goody-goody side of Dickie effectively enough. He quickly corrected this by altering his smile accordingly and saying: 'Thank you. I hope you don't mind me taking up your time like this.'

'No. No, that's fine.' Penny blinked and looked again at the photocopy. Any hint of nastiness that may previously have been on his face was now completely gone. This was the Dickie that Penny knew. (The photocopy was convincing because, like most evil creatures, he was able to be nice and appear good when it fitted in with his twisted plans.)

Penny shrugged her shoulders, and put her recent uneasiness down to an overactive imagination after a tiring day at school. Why was she worrying? She was safe with Dickie, wasn't she? Of course she was.

She patted the photocopy on the back and urged: 'Come on, then. The river's down that way.'

Yes, Penny was perfectly safe with harmless Dickie Dustbin. But this wasn't Dickie Dustbin that she was with—at least, not the side of Dickie that she knew.

Not much later the side of Dickie that Penny *did* know found himself being carried along somewhere in Jonathan's arms. He had nodded off when Jonathan left him in the woods, but now he'd woken up.

'Uh...what's going on?' he croaked, clasping his forehead because his head still ached. 'Where are we going?'

'Ah, awake now are we?' puffed Jonathan, stubbornly marching towards his destination. 'Well, Dickie, it looks like you were right about Penny being in danger. I'm taking you to Penny's mum's where the police should be arriving any moment. You're going to be needed to describe this "thing" that attacked you.'

'The "thing"? Oh no.' Dickie groaned as he remembered the black-and-white likeness of him that had knocked him out in the woods, and his head throbbed even more. Dickie had changed a lot in the last few hours. Gone were all the bad thoughts that he used to have about people: the hate, the resentment, the jealousy. Now he loved *everyone*. He even loved the thing that had attacked him, despite all of its nastiness, and that love made him feel worse. Someone Dickie *loved* had hurt him. This sort of rejection was more than he could cope with, and he closed his eyes to try and forget about it all.

Meanwhile, Dickie's likeness and Penny had reached an unglamorous part of the river which few people visited. The riverbank was overgrown with weeds and similar wild stuff, and there were pesky flies everywhere.

Waving away some of the flies, Penny asked: 'So what do you want to know?'

'Give us a kiss!'

'What?'

'Come on. Let's have a snog.'

The photocopy was no longer trying to seem nice. He now appeared quite the opposite, and he tightly clenched his fists, ready to use them violently if he didn't get his way.

Penny was scared. 'What was that, Dickie? I...I've never heard you talk this way before. It's....'

'Shut up, woman! I've had enough of your sickening niceness,' the photocopy snarled hatefully. 'You and Jonathan, with your perfect teeth and blow-dried hairstyles, make me want to puke. Come here. Give us a kiss!'

Penny gasped. 'Dickie, what's come over you?' she demanded. 'I've never seen you like this before. You're not acting like your real self.'

'Ignorant cow!' The photocopy grabbed her violently by the arms, squeezing them tightly. '*I'm* the real Dickie Dustbin, do you hear? I've been hidden deep inside him for years, but finally I've managed to break free.'

The photocopy may have broken free, but unfortunately Penny was not having the same success. No matter how much she struggled, she just couldn't escape from the photocopy's painful grip.

'Owch, let me go,' she squealed, but the photocopy ignored her, leaning forward instead to try and kiss her.

'No, don't you dare,' Penny feebly pleaded. Tears came to her eyes as she jerked her head sideways to avoid his cold, unfeeling lips. 'Leave me alone. You're horrible.'

'So, the truth's coming out now. You've always thought I'm horrible, haven't you?'

'No, that's not true. I....'

'Let me tell you something, woman. You're a pain in the neck. You've always looked down on me; don't tell me you haven't. And you're going to make it up to me by letting me have a good snog.'

'Mmm mmph mm,' mumbled Penny, who this time hadn't managed to avoid the black-and-white lips. Thinking quickly, she nutted him on the forehead then bit down hard on his nose.

'Aaaah!' screamed the photocopy, recoiling in pain. He rubbed his aching nose and blood came off in his hand.

'Look what you've done.' He held out his shaking hand to show that black-and-white blood was dripping between his fingers. 'You've drawn blood from me, and no one does that to me...ever!'

He slapped her so hard on the cheek that she fell to the ground. Naturally, she burst into tears.

'And no one cries in front of me either,' fumed the photocopy, slapping her again.

Cautiously, Penny looked up, fear in her eyes, dirt in her hair, and grimy tears streaking her face. There were deep red marks on her cheek where the photocopy had slapped her.

'Wh-why are you doing this to me, Dickie?' It was hard for her to speak because she was trembling so much. 'What have I done to deserve this sudden hatred from you?' She rubbed her eyes because the tears were blurring her vision, but new tears soon came in their place.

'You've never let me have my way with you,' the photocopy snapped. 'You've been flirting with Jonathan all this time, but not with me. Well, I'm not going to let you get away with it any more. I'm going to have my way with you, woman, whether you want me to or not.'

He pulled Penny up by the hair and slobbered again all over her lips. Penny wasn't going to stand for any more of this. Even though she was weak and confused, she summoned up as much inner strength and self-determination as she could and landed a mighty blow in the photocopy's stomach, just when he wasn't prepared for it.

'Oof!' he went, completely winded and bent double in agony. Light grey tears fell from his eyes.

Taking full advantage of the photocopy's temporary helplessness, Penny fled down the riverbank, turned left at the bridge, ran with all her might down a quiet Walbridge street, then leaped round a corner and found herself in the path of a speeding police car.

'Ulp.' Penny froze in shock in the middle of the road, and the police car quickly swerved, narrowly missing her. As soon as the car had stopped, out jumped two policemen, Penny's mum and good old Jonathan. Penny, realising what was happening, breathed a big sigh of relief. These people were here to help her; they were her friends. Her ordeal was over. She was safe.

She was just about to thank them all for coming to rescue her when, to her horror, she spied Dickie Dustbin sitting in the back seat of the car. Her heart skipped a beat. How on earth did *he* get there? This was like a nightmare that was never-ending.

'Help me!' Penny cried out to the sky.

And then she fainted.

A black car was parked outside Truscott's newsagent's in Walbridge. Inside sat a man wearing a smart black hat, black-framed mirror sunglasses and a black overcoat. He looked impatiently down at his digital wristwatch which wasn't the slightest bit black—but then no one's *totally* consistent, are they?

'Hmm. Five-fourteen,' the man announced to the windscreen (which was a bit silly because windscreens can't hear anything). 'She should be along here any moment now, just like she is *every* Monday at five-fourteen.'

Sure enough, the 'she' he was referring to soon made her usual dramatic appearance. *'She'* was Charlie Digestives' highly eccentric maid, Ethel, and she was skateboarding down the street with a crash helmet on her head and cricket pads on her legs. Ethel had picked up quite a speed, and people all down the street had to jump out of her way as she zoomed along at twice the speed of sound towards the newsagent's.

Once she'd reached her destination, she dismounted from her skateboard, shouted, 'Sorry everyone!' to all the people she'd passed—many of them lying on the pavement with shopping on the floor around them and skateboard marks on their clothes—then stepped inside the newsagent's to purchase the latest issue of *The Beano*, twenty Sherbet Fountains and a giant bottle of Vimto. (This was a weekly ritual for her. Every Monday evening, when her day's work was done, she would put her feet up and read that week's issue of *The Beano*, scoffing an entire Sherbet Fountain after every page and taking frequent gulps from the Vimto bottle to quench her thirst.)

The man from the black car stood by the entrance of the newsagent's, ready to meet Ethel once she'd bought her precious supplies. His dark outfit and impenetrable mirror sunglasses made him look very mysterious.

'Excuse me, Madam,' he said to Ethel when she stepped back outside. 'Are you by any chance Charlie Digestives' maid, Ethel?'

'Yes, that's me,' she admitted. 'What do you want? You'd better make it quick, sonny.' She was dying to find out what happened in the latest *Beano*, and was therefore in a rush to get back home.

'I'm an agent from the ACME Peace Corporation,' revealed the man, 'and I've been asked by Charlie Digestives to take you to him at a secret location in Walbridge. He is taking care of some important business there, and he urgently needs your assistance.'

'Secret location? Important business? Urgently needs my assistance?' Ethel wondered what this important business could be. Maybe Charlie was being attacked by hundreds of man-eating crocodiles, and he urgently needed Ethel to help fight them off. Maybe Charlie was trapped in a cage full of slimy poisonous snakes, and he desperately wanted Ethel to pick the lock of the cage with one of the hairpins in her wig. Or he could be about to embark on a secret journey around the world for the ACME Peace Corporation, and he was going to ask Ethel to travel with him as his bodyguard. True, Ethel wasn't as strong as most bodyguards, but she had in her possession a highly efficient and well concealed weapon: her ultra-sharp, battery-operated dentures which were feared by hardened criminals throughout the land. Charlie Digestives could trek round the world without fear, knowing that Ethel and her dentures were by his side to protect him.

'Golly, how exciting,' thought Ethel. 'Charlie wants me to help him on a case.' She waggled her ears because she was looking forward to her imminent adventure with Charlie. She also flapped her arms up and down because she thought that this, along with her ears waggling, would make her fly. No such thing happened. Maybe it was because the weight of her crash helmet, the Vimto bottle and the twenty Sherbet Fountains was holding her down.

'So, if you'll just step into my car,' urged the supposed agent, 'I'll drive you to him straight away.'

Ethel did as she was told and eagerly climbed into the car. Then, as the 'agent' sat down next to her and turned the key in the ignition, she thought: 'Hang on a mo. Haven't I heard that man's voice somewhere before?' She cast her mind back to when Charlie Digestives made her dress up like a clothes line post, just over a year ago. 'The Clothes Line Snatcher?' She stared closely at the man's features. 'No, it can't be,' she told herself. 'That was ages ago and no one has seen him since. Why should he suddenly turn up now?'

But Ethel was wrong. Yes, you've guessed it, reader. The man driving Ethel to the 'secret location' *was* the Clothes Line Snatcher, in a different costume. He smiled a sinister smile because Ethel was now in his grip and so the next stage in his plan to take over the universe (or rather, universes), and also to take revenge on Charlie Digestives, had successfully been completed. After all his months of planning and waiting, his dire and dastardly scheme would at last be unleashed on a helpless, unsuspecting world.

'Hee hee hee,' he cackled evilly to himself, quietly so that Ethel couldn't hear him. But Ethel wouldn't have heard him even if he shouted at the top of his voice. She was totally engrossed in this week's adventures of Lord Snooty and his pals in *The Beano*, and the sherbet from one of her Sherbet Fountains was getting everywhere.

The Clothes Line Snatcher made a mental note to hoover the inside of the car tomorrow morning after he had completely altered the fabric of the universe and become world leader.

'Alter the fabric of the universe?' I hear you say. 'How's he going to do that?'

Read on and find out, adventure fans. Things are about to hot up!

16

Poor Dickie Dustbin was shattered. He had been gazing out of the police car window for ages now and he had just about had enough.

'Can we have a rest, please?' he requested from the back seat of the car, much fatigue evident in his feeble voice. 'My head's still throbbing, I've had a really intense day, and I don't know how much longer I can watch for my imposter without a break.'

'I agree,' put in Jonathan, also on the back seat. 'Since we dropped Penny and her mum back at their house, we've been driving round Walbridge for almost two-and-a-half hours. Can't we stop for a while? You can only concentrate for so long, you know.'

The policeman in the passenger seat refused to give in.

'I'm sorry, lads,' he insisted. 'Dickie's imposter is still on the loose, and from what you've all told me he's highly dangerous and could strike violently at any moment. We must continue with our search until we apprehend him.'

The policeman who was driving, however, thought differently.

'I agree with the boys,' he informed his colleague, chewing a Curly Wurly while steering round a corner. 'I'm tired myself, driving round the same old streets over and over again. I think we would all benefit from a temporary change of scenery.'

Dickie grunted in agreement, and the policeman continued: 'How about the McDonald's in Ridsdale Street? I desperately need some new food supplies to keep me going. All I've got left under my helmet is three scotch eggs, a box of Maltesers, two bacon and marmalade sandwiches and a Pepsi.' (The two policemen, in case you hadn't already guessed, were the same policemen who were involved in the ill-fated chase for the Clothes Line Snatcher all those months ago.)

'All right, all right,' gave in the first policeman. 'The three of you can have a short break if you want to, I suppose.' There was a cheer from Dickie and Jonathan at his announcement.

'But,' he cautioned, turning round to face the youths at the back, 'may it be on your consciences if Dickie's imposter strikes while we're selfishly stuffing our faces.'

Ding-dong! The front door opened.

'Ah, hello, Professor. Thanks for dropping by. Come on in, and I'll take your coat.'

The location: Charlie Digestives' house in Walbridge. The professor: Professor Alfred Boggles, of course! The man offering to take his coat: Charlie

Digestives, top detective for the famous ACME Peace Corporation. The reason for their get together this evening: to talk about the meaning of life.

'Vere iss Ethel at der moment?' Professor Boggles asked, while Charlie hung his coat on a rack in the hallway. 'She's der von who normally answers der door.'

'I don't know,' Charlie admitted, leading the professor into the living room. 'When I got back from all my crime-solving activities today she wasn't at home. She could have gone down the road to Bernie's Bingo Emporium, I suppose. Or maybe her trampolining lessons started tonight.'

'Hmm, very odd. Very odd indeed. It's not like your Ethel to leave der house vithout writink you a note or tellink you vere she's off to.'

'Don't worry, Professor. I'm sure she's all right. Take a seat, and I'll get the Tizer and Twiglets from the kitchen.'

Professor Boggles did as he was told and made himself comfortable in the armchair by the window. The room was in quite a chaotic state, but that came as no surprise to him; Charlie's living room was always in a mess. There were the usual newspapers and comics strewn about the floor, records and CDs in an untidy pile by the hi-fi, bits everywhere of a 2,000 piece jigsaw of Cliff Richard that Charlie started years ago and soon gave up on, and Bob Monkhouse posters stuck crookedly on the walls all round the room. (Bob Monkhouse was Charlie's favourite comedian. He never missed him when he was on the telly. Charlie thought he was brill.) Also in the living room were hundreds and hundreds of milk bottles, containing different amounts of water.

Professor Boggles scratched his scientific head,

puzzled at the presence of all the milk bottles, then noticed that there was a country bumpkin standing next to the telly in front of him, dressed in smelly farm clothes and chewing a piece of straw. To the right of him was a tall mound of photographs of tractors—tractors of every conceivable size, shape and colour. For some reason he was bitterly ripping each photo into lots of tiny pieces. He looked quite narked, and every few seconds he was angrily exclaiming words like 'Ooh ar!' or 'Fertiliser!'

'Hello dere, mein goodt man. Vot exactly are you doink?' the professor was about to ask him, but he never got the chance because Charlie walked into the room at that precise moment, holding a tray with a bowl of Twiglets on it and two tall glasses full to the top with Tizer and ice cubes. Placing the tray on the coffee table, Charlie smiled and said: 'I expect you're wondering what all these milk bottles are doing in here.'

'Vell, I, erm...'

'Another one of Ethel's odd projects, I'm afraid. There's going to be a concert at the old people's home next month, and Ethel and a few of her friends there have decided to perform Handel's *Messiah* in its entirety on milk bottles, tapping them with spoons to get the right notes. I can't see that it'll work, to be honest with you.'

'But, der...'

'Come on, Professor. Eat up those Twiglets. You love them, don't you? And I'll tell you why I need your advice.'

Professor Boggles was desperate to know why that country bumpkin was standing next to the telly, ripping up the photos. But instead of asking Charlie about it, he patiently listened to his friend explain why he'd been doing all this deep thinking lately. Charlie told him about the experience he'd had on the morning of the destruction of the 'Wow' Screen—that unexpected reassuring sensation that some wonderful being who was mind-bogglingly powerful loved and accepted him totally. He also told the professor about the smiling figure in the white robe that he'd seen on the stage of the Walbridge Museum lecture hall—and that he felt as if he were in the presence of a king or a prime minister. Nothing like that had happened to him since then, but the two experiences had been constantly on his mind.

'I know now that there's more to life than meets the eye,' continued Charlie. 'More to life than just the world around us and everyday things. And now that I've had a taste of that I want to know more. But how? Who is this being who's bigger than us and who's in the process of sorting out the mess the world's in. And that man in the robe: who was he, and why was I the only one who saw him?'

Professor Boggles thought for a moment then shrugged his shoulders. 'I'm not sure I can help you, Charlie,' he admitted. 'I'm chust ass much in der dark about dese sorts off thinks ass you are, I'm afraid. I'm a scientist. Mein job iss to figure out how thinks in der universe vork. Vot I can't tell you iss who—if anyvon—made dem, and *vy* dey vere made.'

Charlie looked desperately disappointed. 'So who *can* tell me, then?' he demanded. 'I really need to know.'

The professor didn't like seeing his friend troubled like this, but for all his scientific knowledge he just didn't know what to say. Luckily he didn't have to think of anything because the hallway phone rang at that point. Charlie went to answer it, and he soon returned to the living room with a troubled expression on his face.

'Vot's up, Charlie?' Professor Boggles asked him.

Charlie looked grave. 'That was the Clothes Line Snatcher on the phone,' he revealed. 'He says he's kidnapped Ethel, and he's going to do something extremely nasty and horrible to her unless I rescue her.'

'Vot?'

'I said, "He's kidnapped Ethel, and he's going to do something extremely nasty and horrible to her unless I rescue her." Didn't you hear me?'

'Nein, you misunderstandt me. Mein "Vot?" voss a shocked exclamation; not a reqvest for you to repeat yourself.'

'Oh, sorry.' With more than a hint of panic in his voice, Charlie then added: 'Anyway, we must hurry to save her. If it *was* the Clothes Line Snatcher who called, she's in great danger.'

'Vere iss she?'

'29 Lottbridge Drive. Come on, get your coat on quick. We've got to act fast.'

'Off course.' Professor Boggles obediently jumped from the armchair and hurried towards the hallway. He stopped in mid-step when he remembered the country bumpkin who was still angrily ripping up the photographs of tractors.

'Just von kvestion before ve leave,' the professor requested.

'What's that?'

'Vy iss dat man dere by der telly?'

'Mr Sproggins, you mean?' Charlie quickly glanced in his direction. 'Ethel brought him back

136

when I told her to get us something for all the hot weather we've been having.'

'Fertiliser!' cursed Mr Sproggins in the background.

Professor Boggles looked dumbfounded. 'I don't see der connection betveen him undt der hot veather,' he admitted.

'Well,' said Charlie, 'you know how Ethel often misunderstands me when I ask her to get me things. This time I asked her for an extractor fan.'

The professor didn't understand. 'An extractor fan? But vot hass dat got to do vith...?' And then it hit him. 'Off course! Ethel dussn't get any better, duss she? She thought you vonted somevon who used to like tractors. Giggle undt chortle!'

Professor Boggles found this so amusing that he chuckled all the way to Charlie's car outside. But Charlie didn't laugh at all; the downhearted expression on his face showed that even the greatest comedians in the world wouldn't have made him laugh tonight—not even Bob Monkhouse. He was worried about the awful things that would happen to poor Ethel if they arrived too late. They mustn't waste a second.

'Hee hee hee,' cackled the Clothes Line Snatcher in his small viewing room at 29 Lottbridge Drive. Like all villains in movies and comic books he could somehow see everything his adversaries were doing on television screens (villains can be clever sometimes), and he was currently watching Charlie and the professor speeding towards his hideout. 'My hated enemy, Charlie Digestives, is heading straight for my hideous evil trap which is really nasty, even by my standards. And it looks like Professor Boggles will soon be in my grip as well. What a pleasant surprise!' Not so pleasant for the professor, though.

The Clothes Line Snatcher was no longer dressed as a mysterious agent from the ACME Peace Corporation. Now he was dressed to look like the school caretaker of Heathlands Secondary School, which was actually quite easy for him because he *was* the school caretaker. He'd had the job almost a year now (he got it just after his jump through the 'Wow' Screen), and he'd disguised his voice with a lisp all these months so that people wouldn't recognise who he really was.

'Hee hee hee,' he cackled again. (He seems to cackle 'Hee hee hee' rather a lot, doesn't he? I hope he doesn't do it many more times otherwise it's going to get tedious.)

Ethel, tied securely to a chair in the viewing room, also went 'Hee hee hee', not because she was looking forward to the Clothes Line Snatcher capturing Charlie and Professor Boggles—far from it. No, she went 'Hee hee hee' because she was excited that she had been kidnapped and that Charlie and the professor were coming to her rescue. This was all a big adventure for her.

The Clothes Line Snatcher didn't like Ethel enjoying herself while she was his prisoner. This just would not do.

'Shut up, woman!' he screamed. 'Why are you laughing? You're supposed to be scared. After all, I've threatened to do all sorts of horrible things to you.'

'I see,' said Ethel. 'You want me to scream and beg and plead for mercy.'

'Yes, please. That would be nice.'

'Okay.' Ethel let out a high-pitched scream that

almost burst the Clothes Line Snatcher's eardrums, and then she pleaded, 'Oh, do please let me go, Mr naughty Clothes Line Snatcher, sir. I'm very frightened, you know. Mercy, mercy, and other stuff like that.' Ethel was enjoying this 'pleading for mercy' business; it was quite a laugh. She went 'Hee hee hee' again because she hadn't had so much fun in ages.

The Clothes Line Snatcher groaned, but he comforted himself with the realisation that she—as well as Charlie Digestives and the professor—would soon be out of his way once he had taken his revenge on them all.

'Hee hee hee,' he cackled evilly. (Not again.)

Penny Green moaned as she slowly opened her eyes and adjusted them to the glare of the lightbulb in her room. She was lying awkwardly in her bed, and when she turned she saw that her parents were in the room with her. Her mum was knitting, and her dad was chewing the end of a pencil while deciding how to fill in his pools coupon. Actually, he'd stopped working on the pools coupon a few seconds before. Now he was looking at Penny because he'd heard her moan. He nudged Penny's mum in the ribs.

'What, dear?'

'It's Penny, love. Look, she's stirring.'

'Penny? Oh, yes, Malcolm. You're right.' She leaned over the bed and looked into her daughter's eyes. 'How are you doing, Penny?'

'Where am I?'

'In your room. You're safe now. Everything's all right.'

'But...the police car. And Dickie.'

'It's *all right*, Penny.' This was her father speaking

now. 'You had a bit of a fright when the police car nearly hit you. But you're home now.'

Penny had vague, distant memories of her mum carrying her up the stairs when the police had dropped them back at their house. After that she must have gone straight to sleep.

'And as for Dickie's imposter,' added Penny's mum, 'Jonathan, the police and Dickie, are on his trail right now. He won't get in here to frighten you any more, dear; we'll make sure of that.'

'Imposter? What do you mean?'

Her father was the one who answered. 'Dickie explained it to me when the police dropped you off. He reckons that a black-and-white replica of himself came into being after a special liquid created by Professor Boggles soaked through a photocopy of his face. Dickie thinks that everything in him that was evil and nasty is now in the photocopy version of himself, leaving him totally pure and good. The person who attacked you wasn't Dickie; it was the replica.'

This made sense to Penny. 'No wonder he looked so pale,' she thought. She was still very fond of Dickie, and she was glad that he wasn't to blame. The real Dickie would never have treated her the way his photocopy had by the river.

Relief and a strong sense of peace came with this new information, and Penny's eyes slowly closed again. Her traumatic encounter with Dickie's replica—as well as all her worrying about whether she and Jonathan should jump through the 'Wow' Screen again—had drained her emotionally. She was exhausted.

'That's it, love,' encouraged her mum, seeing that she was dropping off to sleep again. 'You have a good rest.' She tucked Penny's blankets tightly around her, then looked across at her husband.

Her husband, knowing what she was thinking, nodded at her then announced to Penny: 'Now that we know you're all right, Mum and I are going downstairs. If you want anything, just give us a shout and we'll come straight up.'

Penny yawned, and was about to tell her parents how much she loved them when she slid quickly back into unconsciousness. Her mum and dad smiled at each other, kissed each other on the cheeks, then left Penny alone in her room.

Penny tossed and turned in her bed, grunting as if she was in pain. She was having a horrible dream that her friend Dickie Dustbin was in terrible danger. I believe they call it feminine intuition.

17

'Are you sure diss iss der place?'

'Of course, Professor. 29 Lottbridge Drive. This is where the Clothes Line Snatcher told me to come.'

Charlie Digestives and Professor Boggles were standing outside a small brown house in Walbridge. They couldn't tell it was brown because it was dark outside at the moment, but I know it was brown because I've seen it myself in the daylight. There are also some nice daffodils in the front garden, a nice goldfish pond round the back, and some grotty garden gnomes seated round it which are not so nice. (In case you wanted to know. Sorry if you didn't.)

'Okay, den.' The professor pressed the front doorbell, and Charlie clenched his fighting fists, ready to use them in case there was any danger.

Both of them were tense all over, ready to run, attack, or do anything else that was needed once the Clothes Line Snatcher had answered the door. Professor Boggles was even prepared to do his famous impersonation of a panicking chicken riding an out-of-control motorbike (always a hit at parties that the professor was invited to, and the professor was invited to lots of parties). After some consideration, however, he realised that maybe his impersonation wouldn't be appropriate right now. They were about to confront a dangerous foe they had been after for more than a year now. Who knew what deadly surprise would be waiting for them behind that door? This was definitely not the time for fun and games.

There was no immediate answer to the doorbell, so Professor Boggles rang it again. Again, no answer.

'You must haff been wrong, Charlie,' said the professor. 'Dere's no von here.'

'Very strange,' said Charlie, disappointedly. 'I could have sworn he told me 29 Lottbridge Drive.'

They turned to walk back up the garden path, but stopped when they heard a loud creaking noise behind them. They turned back round and gasped when they saw that the front door was slowly opening by itself. (This would have been even more scary if a bright flash of lightning had loudly cracked and lit up the sky at just the right time—but nothing of the sort happened. Neither was it raining, and it was inappropriately warm instead of spine-tinglingly cold. Nature can be so unco-operative at times.)

142

Exchanging worried glances, Charlie and the professor bravely stepped into the hallway and heard what was unmistakably the Clothes Line Snatcher's voice coming from somewhere upstairs.

'Good evening, Charlie Digestives,' the voice sneered down the stairs. 'It's me, your dreaded enemy, the Clothes Line Snatcher. It's a pleasure to meet up with you again; a pleasure for me, that is, but not for you—as you and Professor Boggles will soon find out. Hee hee hee.' (There he goes again.)

'But enough of this informal banter,' the Snatcher continued. 'Let's get down to business, shall we? Ethel's with me here upstairs, and I really don't think she's going to last for much longer. Why don't both of you come up here and rescue her?'

'What are you doing to her, you beast?' Charlie yelled, peering anxiously up the stairs for a glimpse of his long-lost foe. His peering was unfruitful. Nothing could be seen round the bend that led to the top—not even the Clothes Line Snatcher's shadow. All he could see was thick, intimidating darkness.

'What I'm doing to her,' the Snatcher answered, 'is so indescribably horrible that it's impossible for me to recount it to you because, as I've just said, it is indescribable.'

While Charlie puzzled over the logic behind the Clothes Line Snatcher's confusing last sentence, Professor Boggles curiously fingered the long strength of string attached to the inside door handle. The string led all the way up the stairs, and Professor Boggles shuddered when he realised that the Clothes Line Snatcher was almost sure to be on the other end of it. This deadly villain had obviously tugged at it to open the door.

'Should ve risk it, Charlie?' he questioned, shaking because he was nervous. 'Who knows vot dreadful fate might befall us if ve go up dose stairs.'

'Of course we should risk it!' Charlie snapped at his cowardly colleague. 'Ethel's in danger, and she needs our help. What are you—a chicken?'

This would have been the perfect cue for Professor Boggles to do his impersonation of a panicking chicken riding an out-of-control motorbike, but he resented Charlie calling him a chicken and the last thing he wanted to do was confirm his accusation.

His pride had been attacked, so he snorted defiantly: 'Me, a chicken? No vay! I'm goink up dose stairs to rescue your Ethel!'

Charlie smiled—he'd hoped this would be the professor's reaction—and the two of them bravely tiptoed up the stairs. They both held their breath anxiously as they turned round the bend near the top to see:

Nothing. It was totally dark up there. All the lights were out.

'Help me! I'm scared of the dark!' pleaded Ethel from somewhere in the distance.

'Don't worry, Ethel. We're coming to help you!' Charlie shouted back. He and the professor cautiously advanced along the upstairs corridor, then turned into the room where they thought they'd heard her voice.

'Over here. That's right. In the corner.' It was Ethel again.

'Everything's going to be all right,' Charlie whispered loudly to reassure her. 'You'll be out of here soon.'

Their hearts beat ever faster as they progressed further into the room. They couldn't see where they were going, or if there was anyone else in there with them. They were only too painfully aware that the Clothes Line Snatcher could strike at any moment.

'Please hurry,' urged Ethel. 'The Snatcher wants to trap you in this cage with me, and he's...mmm mmf.'

Charlie and the professor froze in their tracks, mere inches from where they reckoned Ethel was. The Clothes Line Snatcher must have put his hand over Ethel's mouth to stop her from revealing more of his plan. That meant that he was in the same room, just a few steps away. What should they do?

Before they had time to react, Ethel screamed: 'Watch out! He's going to...!' Then they each felt a cold hand pushing them forward, and there was a loud 'clank' as the cage door shut firmly behind them. Charlie swiftly jumped back round and tugged at the cage door with all his might. It didn't take him long to realise that they were well and truly trapped.

'Clothes Line Snatcher! Where are you?' Charlie fumed through the bars. He was furious. 'You're not going to get away with this, do you hear?'

The Clothes Line Snatcher didn't answer him. Instead there was another 'Hee hee hee' (surprise surprise) as he marched out into the corridor and slammed the door shut. Then they heard him running down the stairs. Now that he had the three of them in his possession, he obviously had other business downstairs that he needed to attend to.

'Mein goodness,' gasped the professor, his teeth loudly chattering because he was scared. 'Ve've been caught. Diss iss terrible. Vot are ve goink to do? Undt vot's der Clothes Line Snatcher goink to do to *us*?'

Charlie felt his way round to Ethel's side of the cage (which didn't take him long because they were in a very small cage), and he discovered that Ethel was tied to a chair. He loosened the rope that bound her, while she happily enthused: 'Fun this, innit! Thanks for coming to rescue me, sir. It's a shame we're all trapped here like this, but I'm sure you'll find some way for us to escape.'

Charlie was annoyed that Ethel didn't realise how grave their situation was; she could be infuriatingly ignorant at times. He was also, however, flattered by her confidence in him, although he wasn't sure that he could live up to her high expectations.

'Yes, we're going to escape. Of course we are,' he said to encourage Ethel and the professor, but he didn't really believe it. He wasn't going to accept defeat too easily, though, so he set about methodically feeling each bar of the cage to try and find any weak points.

The front doorbell rang frequently in the next half-hour or so, and more and more people could be heard in a room downstairs, chatting away while chart music played in the background. Charlie reckoned that some sort of party was going on, and he was right. It was the school caretaker's party, and it was taking place in his living room.

More than thirty people showed up for the party, including Crusher and his gang. Crusher had just been suspended indefinitely from Heathlands School because of his punch-up with Dickie Dustbin, so he wasn't in the best of moods. (Even when he *was* in the best of moods, he still wasn't very likable). His gang were huddled closely together in one corner of the room, loudly snarling with anger at their leader's humiliation. Secretly some of them were pleased that Crusher had been punished like this because they didn't really like him too much. However, they didn't let on that they felt this way, otherwise Crusher would have duffed them up.

Also at the party was Mr Hobbs, the Religious Education teacher, staring glumly down into his glass of punch and stubbornly refusing to talk to anyone. He looked thoroughly miserable, which wasn't too surprising because that was how he normally looked. Standing next to him was a brickie from down the road who didn't have a kind word to say about anyone, and whose main motto in life was, 'You've got to look after number one.' (Sometimes when he wanted to impress people, he'd say, 'You've got to look after numero uno,' which I think is Italian, although I may be wrong.)

Elsewhere in the room was a journalist from the *Walbridge Herald* who was of the opinion that the whole world was totally rotten and that his main purpose in life was to expose all that rottenness in his articles. He was talking to Nora Nodules, lead singer for Chemical Warfare, a local punk rock group. Chemical Warfare's songs dealt mostly with death and violence and other unpleasant subjects like that. Nora looked as if she was dressed for a funeral; all her clothes were black, and there was white powder all over her face which made her look half-dead herself. Nora hadn't smiled for years. Life to her was just one big drag.

It was pretty obvious that everyone who had come to the party had one thing in common: a deep hatred and bitterness in their lives which made them thoroughly unpleasant people to be with. Surprisingly, none of those at the party realised they had this similarity with each other; they were too wrapped up in their private and often self-inflicted miseries to notice how anyone else was feeling.

147

The school caretaker with a lisp (really the Clothes Line Snatcher, remember?) faded down the music in the background and stood at the front of the living room. He cleared his throat loudly to show that he wanted everyone to stop talking and listen to him.

'Thank you all for thowing up here tonight,' he eventually said when there was silence in the room, 'and I hope you're all enjoying yourthelveth.'

'Enjoy myself? Here?' muttered one ungrateful chap, a prominent member of the local borough council. 'I could have more fun watching a snail decompose.'

Mrs Hawkfield, an unfulfilled housewife who lived next door, was similarly ungrateful. She began complaining about 'the appalling taste of the punch', but the caretaker cut her short by announcing: 'Now, before we continue, I jutht want to thow you all an ingeniouth new contrapthion that wath given to me by thomeone I love very much.'

Some in the room yawned; others looked generally apathetic. None seemed the slightest bit interested in seeing the caretaker's 'ingenious new contraption'.

The caretaker didn't mind everyone's apparent lack of interest—it meant that they didn't suspect what he was about to do. Smiling wickedly, he unexpectedly whipped out a gun-like device from inside his jacket and quickly shot what looked like a bright red laser ray at all the ungrateful party-goers. They all froze immediately where they were, totally unconscious but still standing upright and with their eyes wide open.

The school caretaker grinned triumphantly, then ripped off his clothes to reveal his Clothes Line Snatcher outfit underneath. Putting on his black

148

hood to complete the sinister outfit, he sneered (without the lisp now because no one was listening to him): 'Good, my new hypno-ray has worked, and all these morons are helplessly in my grip, ready to do whatever I want them to. Yes, this hypno-ray gun *was* made by someone I love very much...*me!*'

The Clothes Line Snatcher thought that this was hilariously funny, but then it's a well-known fact that all nasty villains have a twisted sense of humour.

Instead of cackling 'Hee hee hee' at this point— which is what I would have expected—he chuckled 'Ho ho ho', which made a very pleasant change indeed.

The Clothes Line Snatcher then set about doing to his helpless guests whatever he needed to in order to achieve his aim of totally altering the fabric of the universe and becoming world leader. Sorry to be so vague about what he actually did to the guests, but I've got to leave questions like this unanswered, haven't I? Otherwise you won't want to read on to find out what happened to them.

Sorry.

I'm only doing my job.

Only a few more pages then all will be revealed....

18

The three of them had been in the cage almost an hour, and they were deadly bored. There wasn't much they could do there in the dark, except maybe examine all the bars to try and find weak points. Charlie had done this twenty times already to every single bar, and he hadn't found any weak points at all.

Ethel tried to amuse herself by repeatedly cracking her nose while humming different tunes from Rodgers' and Hammerstein's *South Pacific*. Ethel was partly successful at amusing herself, but the others in the cage weren't so amused. As forms of percussion go, cracking one's nose every second or so is hardly the most pleasing to the ear. Also, Ethel's humming was dreadfully out of tune, especially on 'Happy Talk' and 'Younger Than Springtime'. And the normally haunting 'Bali Ha'i' was now merely annoying. A shame.

Professor Boggles had been strangely quiet for the last few minutes. He'd been deep in thought, and the question, 'What is the point of all my work?' had been going through his mind over and over again. It bothered him that he hadn't been able to help Charlie back at his house. Charlie had opened up his heart to the professor—had cried out to him for help—and the professor hadn't known what to say. True, he was the one who had single-handedly devised and constructed the spectacular 'Wow' Screen. Yes, he was the one who was developing the almost miraculous liquid that could bring dead plants back to life. And he was also the one who had perfected the world's first (and last) solar-powered torch—but then no loony professor can expect to have a perfect track record with his inventions. (The professor had spent ages working on that torch. He could never figure out why no one had wanted to buy it.)

Professor Boggles was an undisputed genius. He was recognised as one of the foremost thinkers of the worldwide scientific community. Yet, in spite of all his knowledge, he couldn't answer any of the basic questions of life, such as: 'What is the reason I'm alive?' and, 'Am I special and meaningful in this universe, or just an insignificant creature on a planet in some obscure solar system?' Maybe Charlie was right. Maybe there was more to life than just the world around us and everyday things. But if that was the case, just what was it?

Charlie Digestives was also deep in thought. (He was helpless to do anything about their present situation, so there was nothing much else he *could* do.) He was mainly thinking about this business with the man in the white robe and the loving being who was taking care of the mess that the world was in. A gut feeling told him that that being was God, the person who created everything in the first place. And maybe the man in the robe represented God in human form so that we mere humans could understand more what God was like. Whatever the case, Charlie knew that he desperately wanted to meet the man in the robe again. And not just *meet* him—Charlie wanted to spend a lot of time with him, and do with his life whatever the man wanted him to. Charlie suspected that only then would his life have any real meaning.

His thoughts were interrupted by a loud mechanical whirring sound, caused by the cage descending through a hole in the floor to a corner of the living room below. (It descended on a special system of scaffolding, pulleys and wires, just like a lift.) It halted two feet above the floor, and when Charlie looked around he saw lots of hypnotised bodies standing in one big circle around the room, connected to each other by electrical wires which were coming out of what looked like shower caps on their heads. Charlie also saw the Clothes Line Snatcher at the front of the room, grinning maliciously behind his operations console, which looked like a complicated mixing desk in a recording studio.

The Clothes Line Snatcher sneered at the three in the cage: 'Ha! At last, my diabolical plan to alter the fabric of the universe completely and become world leader is about to be put into operation. And none of you can stop me!'

'What heinous scheme have you hatched now, you monster?' demanded Charlie. Ethel and Professor Boggles would have asked this question as well, except that they were both too scared to speak. Ethel had finally realised how serious this whole thing was, and she was so scared that she was biting her fingernails. The professor, who didn't want to ruin his fine fingernails, was biting his beard instead. This was an alternative that, for obvious reasons, was not available to Ethel.

'You want to know my plan?' The Clothes Line Snatcher wondered whether he should answer Charlie's question, and soon decided that he would. He realised that it would give him enormous satisfaction to explain his plan proudly to his three captives before killing them off. This is very convenient, as he'll now be explaining some vital parts of the plot.

'Very well, then, I'll tell you,' the Snatcher obliged. 'I'll be killing you all soon anyway, so my top-secret information will safely die with you.'

'Die with us? Help! We're going to die!' shrieked

Ethel, continuing to bite her fingernails while she was shrieking. 'I'm too young to die!' (Actually, this wasn't strictly true.) 'And I won't be able to see what happens tomorrow in *Neighbours*!'

Professor Boggles was also fear-stricken. 'Donner undt Blitzen! He's goink to kill us!' he cried, and he began biting his toenails instead of his beard. He was obviously very scared.

The only person who put on a brave face was Charlie Digestives, who had faced death many times already in his dangerous career. He looked very stern indeed, and he wasn't impressed by the Clothes Line Snatcher's threats.

The Snatcher, not put off by Charlie's apparent indifference, switched a tape on at his operations console so that eerie church organ music could be heard from loudspeakers around the room. (The tape was called *K-Tel Presents the Best of Eerie Church Organ Music Volume 3*.) He then proceeded with the explanation of his plan, the music making his explanation all the more chilling (which, of course, was the Clothes Line Snatcher's intention).

'My plan. Yes, well, in order for my plan to be fully understood, it is necessary to go back in time a number of years to something that happened in my youth.' The Snatcher went all thoughtful at this point as his mind was transported back to a traumatic event in his childhood.

'Have you ever wondered, Charlie, why I have such a dislike for clothes lines?' he asked, very quietly and seriously.

'Well, yes, actually,' admitted Charlie. 'I....'

The Clothes Line Snatcher continued before Charlie could finish answering. 'Did you ever see *The*

Magic Roundabout?* Do you remember the dog on it called Dougall? Well, I used to have a doll of Dougall. He was my best friend. Schoolfriends and others let you down sometimes, but Dougall dolls *never* let you down—especially mine. Dougall and I were inseparable. I'd take him everywhere with me: to school, to cub scouts on Wednesdays, and to my friend Paul's house whenever I went round to help make our life-size model of Valerie Singleton,** using matchsticks and old Fairy Liquid bottles.

'You know, I even went to bed with Dougall. I'd lay him on the pillow next to me so that if I woke up in the middle of the night he'd be there to reassure me. I loved my Dougall doll, Charlie. I loved him very much.'

'Great. Fantastic,' thought Charlie, sarcastically. 'So you had a doll of Dougall from *The Magic Roundabout*.*** So what? What's that got to do with clothes lines?' Charlie wished that the Snatcher would hurry up and get to the point.

Ethel and Professor Boggles, however, were totally engrossed by the Clothes Line Snatcher's story. They thought it was rather sweet.

'One evening,' continued the Snatcher (the church organ music in the background now sounded sad), 'I made a terrible, terrible mistake. I was so excited about going round to Paul's house—we were due to

---

* *The Magic Roundabout* was a brilliant five-minute children's programme that used to be on the telly quite regularly.
** Valerie Singleton was an early presenter of BBC TV's *Blue Peter*, and quite nice she was too.
*** I like using asterisks. It's fun.

start work on Valerie Singleton's nose—that I forgot to take Dougall with me.

'When I got back home my mum looked very upset, and she said that she had some bad news for me.

' "What's wrong, Mum?" I asked.

' "Son," she admitted, "Dougall is no more."

' "What?"

' "When you were out," she explained, "I put your school blazer in the washing machine. I didn't realise that Dougall was in the inside pocket. And I'm afraid he didn't take too kindly to being spun around in there for so long."

' "Ulp." This was the worst news that I could possibly hear. "So, where...how...?" I barely managed to say through my sobs.

' "He's outside," answered Mum, "or at least what's left of him. He's drying on the clothes line."

'I immediately ran outside. It was not a pretty sight that met me, I can tell you. My precious Dougall, who'd meant everything to me, was now in six soggy, mangled pieces, each one individually pegged up on the clothes line. It was all I could do not to turn away in revulsion. The piece that contained his face was barely recognisable; his normally cheerful features were horribly twisted and distorted in a grotesque parody of his former self. My mum was right: Dougall *was* no more. And I was the saddest boy in all the earth.

'That night my sadness gave way to deep rage. Why did my Dougall have to die? He hadn't done anything wrong to anyone. I couldn't blame my mum—it was a mistake that anyone could have made. But I cursed the forces of the universe for allowing this terrible injustice to happen. I cursed any deity who may be looking down on us for being so unfair. I cursed fate for being so horribly, horribly cruel. And I vowed that I would devote the rest of my life to avenging the senseless death of my Dougall doll. I didn't know *how* I was going to avenge his death—I just knew it was something I had to do.

'After that dreadful day I could never watch *The Magic Roundabout* again. Neither could I bear the sight of clothes lines any more, because every time I saw one it brought to mind the last time I saw Dougall, hideously dismembered and pegged up on my mum's clothes line—a sickening image which has burned itself into my memory for ever, I'm afraid. I especially hated housewives hanging washing on their clothes lines; it was as if they were declaring to me, "I don't care in the slightest what happened to your pathetic Dougall doll, and to prove I don't care I'm going to hang up my washing as normal as if it never happened." Well, I wasn't going to stand for that! To make them all pay I was going to steal all their clothes lines so that they could mock me no more on wash days. What a perfect way to avenge Dougall's death: ridding the whole world of these common-or-garden symbols of my Dougall doll's tragic death.

'I felt nothing but hatred for those housewives. I hated my schoolfriends for not understanding the grief I was going through. Most of them made fun of me, which was so heartless. Needless to say, they weren't my friends for much longer. I hated every single person in the world who insisted on going about their day-to-day business as normal, as if this whole terrible incident was really no big deal—and I hated clothes lines with a vengeance!

'Deep hatred, that's all I've ever felt for anyone

since then—hatred, hatred, *hatred!*' The eerie church organ music got quite angry and deafening at this point, effectively underlining the Clothes Line Snatcher's present state of mind.

Ethel and Professor Boggles were both crying.

'That's so sad,' wept Ethel. 'He lost the only thing in the world that he truly loved.' Ethel could quite identify with the Snatcher's tale of woe. She used to have an Action Man called Doris that she thought the world of. It was a special Action Man with gripping hands. And she had a bazooka gun that went with it so that she could go, 'Kapow! Daka daka! Take that, you filthy rotten thing, you! Eaaaaoooooooooouu... kabloomph!'

Unfortunately, heartless old Charlie had used Doris as bait in 'The Case of the Hairy Things from Space What Eat Action Men', and Charlie didn't catch the hairy things until they'd already eaten Doris' head, most of its torso *and* its special gripping hands. Ethel was so upset, she wouldn't talk to Charlie for a week.

Professor Boggles wailed: 'Sniff! He lost hiss Dougall doll. Dat's even vorse dan der time I accidentally blew up mein model off Brains, mein idol from *Thunderbirds!**' The professor blew his nose into his handkerchief because he was so sad. Ethel blew her nose into the professor's beard because she didn't have a handkerchief.

Charlie Digestives also felt sorry for the Clothes Line Snatcher; he hadn't realised before just how extreme the circumstances were that had led him to his life of wrongdoing. Charlie wondered: if he had

---

* Another old children's television programme.

had the same thing happen to him, would he also be committed to a life of stealing clothes lines? Maybe he would. However, crime *is* crime, two wrongs don't make a right, and no matter how horrible the experience was that the Clothes Line Snatcher had been through, Charlie wasn't going to let him get away with his sinful ways.

'What about forgiveness, Clothes Line Snatcher?'

'Hm? What was that?'

'Forgiveness, Snatcher. You've been carrying all this hatred in your life for years, and it's eating away at you like a cancer. What happened to your Dougall doll all those years ago was bad, and I do sympathise, believe me. But you have to forgive all those you feel have wronged you, otherwise your hatred will grow more intense and you'll be miserable for the rest of your life. Do you honestly want to be miserable for the rest of your life, Clothes Line Snatcher?'

'Pah! How can you expect me to forgive, Charlie? You can't even begin to conceive of the terrors I experienced when seeing my Dougall pegged up on that clothes line. And then to crash through the "Wow" Screen and be helplessly trapped in a strange, intimidating universe, in a body I find repulsive. No, life has been much too cruel to me, Charlie. I don't have to forgive anyone.'

The eerie church organ music became even eerier as the Clothes Line Snatcher started to explain his plan properly.

'Ever since the day I crashed through that screen, I desperately tried to find ways to get back to my universe and into my proper canine body. To finance my various researches, I became caretaker of Heathlands Secondary School, posing as a harmless character with a lisp so that no one would suspect who I really was. It was while on the school playground one day that I got the idea for the plan I am going to carry out tonight.

'I noticed on the playground that the bullies and nasty types—like "Crusher" Craig and his gang— were the ones who always got their way. And the nice, hard working kids—like that wimpy Dickie Dustbin boy—were the ones who got trampled over and pushed around all the time. That got me thinking about the way this world works. It's no good being all loving and good and nice—that's so sickening! The only people who really seem to get anywhere are the hateful ones; those who hate so much that they're willing to climb over anyone who gets in their way in order to get to the top. It's the law of the jungle in this world, Charlie—the survival of the fittest. *And I intend to survive!*

'That night when I got home I decided to try a little experiment. I constructed a special amplifier in my kitchen, then hooked my mind up to it, deliberately remembering all the rotten things that had ever happened to me so that all my anger and hatred and bitterness would rise to the surface. I then turned up the amplifier to full volume so that it magnified my hatred about ten million times, and pointed it at my oven. You'll never guess what happened next, Charlie. The oven glowed bright red, and then disappeared—totally! Actually, this was a bit of a pain at the time because my dinner for that evening was in it—chicken curry, my favourite. But my disappointment at losing my din-dins was soon overshadowed by my excitement at making this important new discovery. Hatred is *much* stronger than love—and maybe that was the key to me getting back to my universe.

'I did some complicated calculations over the next few days, and found that just thirty similarly hateful brains, all hooked up to my amplifier, contained enough power to crack open the universe. And if I cracked the universe open at just the right point, I could get back to the poodle universe. Once there I would have almost unlimited power. With those thirty brains still at my disposal, I could turn deserts into oceans and giant cities into nothing but rubble. I could make planets spin backwards and suns change colour. I could even turn Birmingham City into a decent football team. In short, I could completely alter the fabric of the universe and become world leader!'

The eerie church organ music finished for good as soon as the Snatcher said 'leader!' (what perfect timing), which meant that there was a disconcerting silence in the room as he finally brought his speech to a close. (All nasty villains in books are allowed at least one long speech.)

'So that is what I'm up to tonight, Charlie Digestives. I found thirty of the most hateful people in Walbridge, and invited them round to my house tonight for a party. But, once they were here I hypnotised them all, and now, as you can see, their minds are connected so that all their hatred, multiplied together, can be channelled through my amplifier. The amplifier is under your cage right now, and I have called the ray that will shoot through it my *hate ray*! Before speeding out into the furthest reaches of space, that ray, Charlie, will have to pass through your cage. Its constant barrage of pure, intense hatred will be too much for your feeble body to stand, and within minutes you and your putrid colleagues will be totally disintegrated. It will be an agonising death for you all. What perfect revenge for all the times you've tried to halt my activities!

'Too bad you won't be alive to see my moment of glorious triumph when at last I will be free from this pathetic world of human beings, and I will become world leader!' The Clothes Line Snatcher lifted his hands up high in triumph. He looked pretty pleased with himself. 'Do you hear me, Charlie? I'm going to become *world leader*!'

'Snore!' Charlie and the others in the cage had fallen soundly asleep, using each other as pillows on the grid that was the floor of the cage. The Clothes Line Snatcher's long-winded and boring explanation had gone on for much too long.

'Asleep, eh?' The Snatcher was disappointed; he'd wanted to see them looking mortified at his wonderful plan. 'Well, I'll soon put something through them that'll wake them up all right!'

And he set about making the final adjustments to his equipment for the commencement of his diabolical master plan.

19

A piercing cold night breeze blew through the bars of the cage, slowly waking Charlie from his slumbers.

'No, Sinister Sausage-Lady, don't do that with those gobstoppers,' he mumbled, still half-dreaming, recalling an incident from one of his many past adventures (which will probably turn up in a book some day). 'Phew, Sinister Sausage-Lady, it's freezing out here, isn't it?' he continued mumbling, still half-dreaming.

And then he opened his eyes. 'Hang on a mo,' he said. 'My thrilling showdown with the Sinister Sausage-Lady happened during a heatwave in mid-summer, didn't it? So why did I say it was freezing?'

Charlie discovered the answer to his question when he sat up and surveyed his present surroundings. The cage was now suspended a number of yards above the Clothes Line Snatcher's house, with a spectacular view around it of Walbridge at night; it had gone as high as it could on that system of scaffolding, pulleys and wires. There was a strong breeze blowing outside, and that was why Charlie had said it was freezing. Through the grid beneath his feet he could see a cage-sized hole in the Clothes Line Snatcher's roof. (A square section of the roof must have slid sideways into the rest of the roof to allow the cage to rise through. Ingenious, eh?) There was another cage-sized hole in the floor below, and through this Charlie could see down into the Clothes Line Snatcher's living room where they'd all been subjected to his boring explanation.

Pointing straight up at them from the living room floor was something that looked like a large loud-speaker. At first Charlie wondered what this could be, and then he shivered with fear when he remembered some of the Clothes Line Snatcher's threatening words before he'd dropped off to sleep. That was the hate ray amplifier, wasn't it? If the Snatcher was successful in his devious intentions, any second now the deadly hate ray would be shooting straight up at them, killing them slowly in what the Snatcher had promised would be a horribly painful death.

Charlie wondered whether he should wake up Ethel and Professor Boggles to inform them of his chilling discovery. Eventually he decided not to. There was nothing any of them could do to help themselves now, and the most merciful thing would be to let them continue in their blissful states of unconscious ignorance.

The Clothes Line Snatcher grinned evilly behind the operations console of his now dimly-lit living room. He had deliberately lit it that way so that the atmosphere would be more appropriately menacing for his wicked activities. He counted down from ten—his evil grin growing wider with each passing second—and when he reached zero he expertly flicked a large switch in front of him. Immediately a deep humming sound could be heard from the amplifier. Then, via a microphone at his console, the Snatcher whispered clever suggestions directly into the minds of the hypnotised party-goers around the room. He had obviously done a lot of detailed research into the backgrounds of his specially chosen guests.

'Nora Nodules,' he started, 'cast your mind back to the messy divorce of your parents when you were just seven years old. Remember all the bickering that went on at that time when one of them had reluctantly to look after you. And remember how unloved that made you feel.

' "Crusher" Craig Biggs,' he continued, 'your dad is always criticising you, isn't he? He beats you whenever you do even the slightest thing wrong, and you don't remember him ever saying a nice word about you. You've never felt loved by your parents, and you're totally powerless at home. So you make up for this at school by bullying people who have less strength than you.

'Mr Hobbs, all you've ever wanted is a loving wife and the sound of kids running around your house and calling you "Daddy". But fate has never put you in the path of a suitable woman, so you've been a lonely bachelor for the whole of your life. You've constantly been bitter about your situation over the last few years, and you've taken all your bitterness out on your pupils at school. Now all you've got to look forward to is a long, lonely retirement. You believe there's some sort of god up there, but you're convinced he doesn't care two hoots about you and the rest of the human race—otherwise things maybe would have been better.

'All of you in this room, you all have something in common: at some point in your lives you suffered an extreme injustice which you didn't deserve. Life can be so unfair. I want you all to focus your minds on those injustices, and especially on the hatred those injustices make you feel. That's right. All you feel now is hatred, hatred, *hate!*'

The Snatcher shouted this last word instead of just whispering it, and it seemed to do the trick. The wires connecting everyone's heads suddenly glowed with bright, intense energy, and the humming from the amplifier got steadily louder and more and more high pitched. Soon it got so loud that the Clothes Line Snatcher had to cover his ears—the sound was that unbearable.

Then, just as it became so high pitched that it was impossible for the human ear to hear, there was a startling 'Voomph!' from the amplifier and a deep orange ray shot straight up into space, getting wider the higher it got. Inside the ray were fluorescent green wavy lines, dancing in and out of each other and also heading in the direction of the sky.

'Success!' screamed the jubilant Clothes Line Snatcher, jumping up and down at his operations console. 'My hate ray is working perfectly. Now, if I've aimed it in the right place, it shouldn't be long before this universe cracks open into the poodle universe.'

Up in the cage, Charlie, the professor and Ethel, were writhing around in extreme agony, screaming at the tops of their voices. Almost enough concentrated hatred to crack open the very universe was shooting through their poor, unfortunate bodies. It wouldn't be long before they were totally disintegrated.

As well as heading upwards, hate from the ray was spilling across the floor at a very fast rate. Soon the whole of Walbridge was bathed in a subtle orange glow, and it affected everyone in the town.

Septimus Feeble, the aged town vicar, called his pet hamster a 'twitbag', just for the pure malicious fun of it. He didn't realise he had it in him to be so nasty.

Little Emily Bradshaw flushed her brother's treasured dried worm collection down the loo. She knew he would be heartbroken, but she didn't care. It had taken him ages to build up that collection.

Mr and Mrs Blenkinsop—both of them chartered accountants—wrestled viciously on the living room carpet because they couldn't agree on whether to watch BBC or ITV. They had never had an argument before, and the most vicious thing that Mr Blenkinsop had ever done was savagely bend three paper clips out of shape because he felt a bit rebellious at work. Wrestling like this was not how they normally spent an evening. Most peculiar.

Elsewhere in Walbridge—behind a bush by the river, to be precise—a silent figure who'd been hiding there for the last few hours suddenly stirred as a new source of hatred coursed through his dark grey veins. He hadn't intended to move from his hiding place until well after midnight when no one would be on the streets to find him, but he thrived on hatred and he must have more. Somehow he must find out where all this new hatred was coming from.

The hate ray continued increasing in intensity, and over the next few minutes the Clothes Line Snatcher urged the needle on his hateometer closer to the vital red line. That red line indicated that enough power had been reached to crack open the universe.

'Come on, that's it, just a bit more,' he pleaded with it, but, to his dismay, the needle stopped just micro-millimetres away from the important red line. It remained steady there, and showed no sign of moving closer.

'Curses! I must have miscalculated,' snapped the Snatcher. This was a terrible blow to his plan. 'All I need is just one more person to wire up to my amplifier.'

As if on cue, the photocopy of Dickie Dustbin burst through the living room window. He'd seen the orange ray shooting up into the sky, guessed it must have something to do with the hate all around him, and headed straight for the house it was coming from.

Wiping the broken bits of glass from his clothes (they hadn't hurt him at all), he demanded of the Snatcher, 'Listen, mush, I don't know who you are or what on earth you're playing at here, but if you don't hook me up with that beam of hate, or whatever it is, you're going to be in for it, all right?'

'In for it?'

'That's right, mush!' snarled the photocopy, tightly clenching his fist and thrusting it towards the Clothes Line Snatcher. 'If you don't give me what I want, you're going to regret it!'

The Clothes Line Snatcher wasn't the slightest bit intimidated by the photocopy's threats. Instead he was highly delighted.

'Dickie Dustbin, how wonderful to see you,' he smiled. (Because the light in the room was dim, the Snatcher couldn't tell that the photocopy's skin was black-and-white and that therefore he wasn't the real Dickie Dustbin.) 'Your temperament's changed a bit, I can see, but that's all right. So pleasant to bump into you again. What a shame we can't stop and talk.' He whipped his hypno-ray gun from the holster at his side and pointed it straight at the photocopy's face.

'Oh no you don't,' said the photocopy. Thinking quickly, he retreated hastily to the smashed window and jumped back outside. The Clothes Line Snatcher ran up to the window and poked his head outside, but he couldn't see the photocopy anywhere in the dark Walbridge street. He must be a fast mover.

Just then a police car drove down the street and stopped right outside the Clothes Line Snatcher's house. (Those in the car had spotted the photocopy on the run a few moments ago, and had followed it all the way here.) Two side doors opened, and out jumped Dickie Dustbin and a policeman from the front.

'I don't know; the things I do for you kids,' complained the policeman. (Like most people in Walbridge, he'd been affected by the spillage from the hate ray.) 'I've been chasing around town all night for you ungrateful lot, while I could have been at home with my feet up, sipping a mug of Ovaltine and watching...' He stopped because he was blown away by the sight of the hate ray. 'Bloomin' 'eck!' he said, looking up. 'Do you see that? It looked pretty impressive back there near the river, but here, right up close, it's massive!'

Dickie was also impressed by the sight of the ray, but his first priority was to try and find his double. He was nowhere to be seen.

'That's funny,' Dickie said, scratching his head in a perplexed sort of way. 'I could have sworn that this is the house where he...ulp, who's that man in the window pointing a gun at us?'

The Clothes Line Snatcher didn't waste a second. He shot the hypno-ray gun at Dickie, the policeman *and* the two figures still in the car (Jonathan Matthews and the other policeman). They all froze immediately. The Snatcher then leaped over to Dickie and hauled him through the window into the living room.

'Great,' he said to no one in particular as he hurriedly plonked a 'shower cap' on Dickie's head and attached the relevant wires to it. 'I don't know what's caused this change in Dickie Dustbin, but he's the perfect person now to complete my hate ray circuit.'

He couldn't have been more wrong.

When he was once again behind his operations console, the Snatcher urged all the hypnotised people in the room to concentrate on hateful thoughts. He especially appealed to the new person in the room: 'You hate me, Dickie, don't you? You demanded to be fed on the power from my hate ray, but I denied you that power by zapping you with my hypno-ray gun. Doesn't that just make your blood boil?'

No, it didn't. Deep inside his hypnotised brain, all Dickie could think about was his love for everyone— especially his persistent deep love for Penny Green. This love seeped through his wires to the people next to him, and eventually it flowed through to everyone in the circuit so that they all started thinking nice, lovely thoughts.

The beam emanating from the amplifier was no longer a hate ray—it was now a love ray. And as it shot through the cage above the Snatcher's house, Charlie, the professor and Ethel gradually stopped writhing around in agony as the pain slowly receded and love took over. Eventually they started dancing, laughing and hugging each other while beaming from ear to ear. They were intoxicated in the warm, reassuring glow of the love ray.

'I'm sorry I stole some red ones from your Smartie collection the other day,' Charlie apologised to Ethel; something that he didn't do very often.

'That's all right, sir,' said Ethel, 'and I'm sorry I got cross with you yesterday when you said that horrible thing about Ian McCaskill.' Ian McCaskill, the BBC weatherman, was Ethel's heart-throb. It was her big dream that someday they would get married and spend the rest of their days blissfully identifying cloud formations from the roof of BBC Television Centre or pointing large snooker cues at wall-sized maps of Great Britain.

'Apology accepted, Ethel. I think you're a smashing maid.'

'And you're a smashing boss!'

They hugged each other then, and Charlie kissed Ethel on the cheek. Professor Boggles, meanwhile, happily smiled at the stars around him, imagining he was splitting atoms with his pocket tweezers, or proudly accepting the Nobel Prize for being the best loony professor ever. He had never been happier.

Just like the hate ray, the love ray was spilling out onto the streets and affecting everyone in Walbridge.

The Reverend Septimus Feeble made his pet hamster a cup of tea because he felt bad about calling it a 'twitbag'.

Emily Bradshaw tearfully confessed her sin to her brother, and promised him that first thing tomorrow she'd dig up some new worms for his collection.

And Mr and Mrs Blenkinsop, who couldn't decide on whether to watch BBC or ITV, had come up with a friendly compromise: they were watching a really boring documentary about Venezuelan basket weaving on Channel 4. 'How very fascinating,' said Mr Blenkinsop, and they held hands while cuddling up close on the sofa—something very undignified that they didn't normally do. Right now, though, it just didn't seem to matter.

Penny Green, still in her bedroom, heard Dickie Dustbin's voice calling to her in her mind.

'Penny,' said the voice, 'I need your help—desperately. I love you, Penny; I have for a long time. But I'm in terrible trouble. Please help me. I'm at 29 Lottbridge Drive.'

Penny sat up in bed, deeply disturbed. Why was it she was hearing Dickie's voice in her head? It was because Dickie was unconsciously calling to her through the love ray, but Penny wasn't to know that. All she knew was that she somehow cared for Dickie a lot more than she had before, and she must go to his rescue.

'Help me, Penny,' continued Dickie's voice. 'You must help.'

'I'm coming, Dickie,' promised Penny, and after hastily getting dressed, she quietly sneaked down the stairs and out of the front door without her parents hearing a thing.

The Clothes Line Snatcher was ruthlessly ripping large tufts of hair from his head. The hateometer was registering zero, and he was furious.

'Pathetic!' he bellowed. 'Abysmal! What is going on here? I thought Dickie was going to improve things!'

Suddenly a scream could be heard outside, and the photocopy—who'd been hiding in the rubbish bin in next door's garden—leaped through the living room window. Squirming on the floor, covered in cigarette ashes and smelling of week-old food because of the bin, he pleaded with the Snatcher: 'Turn that beam off! It's killing me! All that love! Phoo! It's awful!'

The Clothes Line Snatcher was confused. 'Dickie?' he said, looking down at the photocopy and then across at Dickie in the circuit. 'How can you be there when you're also connected up to...?' He suddenly paused, looking backwards and forwards between the two of them while deep in thought. Then he shrugged his shoulders and said, 'I don't know why there are two Dickie Dustbins here; I probably never will. All I know is that one of them is like the normal Dickie Dustbin, and the other one's pretty hateful. I reckon the one that's hateful is on the floor.'

'You'd better believe it, mister,' snarled the photocopy, still in pain because of the love ray. 'Now, either turn off that beam, mush, or get it the way it was before.'

The Clothes Line Snatcher grinned. 'With pleasure,' he said, and he shot his hypno-ray gun at the photocopy. 'Your wish is my command.'

With the photocopy now under the Snatcher's control, the ray *would* soon get back to the way it was before. Dickie's love had halted the hate ray temporarily—but it wasn't enough. It was the height of human love, but it clearly wasn't powerful enough to stop the Clothes Line Snatcher's plan.

20

It didn't take long for the Clothes Line Snatcher to remove Dickie Dustbin from the circuit and wire up the hypnotised photocopy in his place. Dickie was now leaning up against the wall by the window, still hypnotised and therefore unaware of everything around him. Which was just as well because what was going on was not very nice.

The Clothes Line Snatcher, after stirring up the emotions of those in the room again—especially the promising new member of the circuit—focused his attention once more on the hateometer, urging the needle forward again as the hate ray resumed its increase in intensity.

Just three minutes and twenty-three seconds later his urging was rewarded. The needle on the hateometer crossed the red line and...BINGO!...enough energy had been reached to crack open the universe.

Which is just what it did.

People all over the world would never forget what happened next. There were deep rumblings throughout the whole planet as if an earthquake was about to happen. There were threatening dark storm clouds everywhere. In the air there was this disconcerting sense that something was not quite right with the way of things.

And then there was a loud thunderclap that shook the whole world—much louder than any noise Concorde ever made—and everywhere suddenly went all blurry with things fading in and out of each other. It was similar to what you see when you cross your eyes and sway from side to side—only in your left eye you can see humans, and in your right eye you can see everyone's poodle equivalent. It was just like a bizarre dream, only those who were seeing it were wide awake.

In the Clothes Line Snatcher's living room there were now twice as many people—or so it seemed. Half of them were humans and half of them were upright poodles, and they were continually sliding in and out of each other, just like the motion of waves washing onto a beach and then pulling out again. It was a sight that would make anyone dizzy. In reality, the human earth and the poodle earth now existed in the same space, but they were slightly out of sync. This is exactly what the Clothes Line Snatcher had intended.

His idea was to turn off the hate ray, hold on tightly to his poodle equivalent (and his poodle equivalent would do likewise because, of course, they were the same person), and then everything would return to normal as the poodle world was sucked back into the right universe like an apple being pulled to earth by gravity. Only, the poodle Clothes Line Snatcher would be back in the right universe in his right body, and vice-versa. Or so he hoped.

But it wasn't to be. When he turned off the amplifier switch, nothing happened—or rather, *everything* was still happening.

'Eh?' he said, not sure why it refused to die down, and he flicked the switch again. Again, nothing changed. In fact, the hate ray was continuing to get more and more intense, and there was no sign of it stopping. The Clothes Line Snatcher hadn't counted on the photocopy's hatred being so strong that it would override all of the controls at his operations console.

The only answer now was somehow to break the hate ray circuit. The Snatcher lunged for a set of wires connecting one head to another, but sparks flew when he touched them. Both of him were thrown back to the floor with the shock—his human body and his poodle body—and they lay there in despair, bitterly disappointed that their plan wasn't working out the way they expected.

As the hate ray continued its barrage on that part of the universe that separates us from the poodle universe, something finally gave way and the damage was irreversible. There was nothing now to separate the poodle universe from the human universe.

All over the world there was the deafening sound of air rushing to fill a vacuum, and then the blurriness, the rumblings and the storm clouds disappeared. Life was normal again...sort of.

Yes, the weather conditions everywhere went

back to how they were a few minutes before. Yes, the ground was now steady again, with no threats of earthquakes. And there was no longer that odd feeling in the air that something was not quite right.

But there was one thing about the planet that was different from the way it was before. There were poodles everywhere. Oodles of them. And they weren't the ghostlike drifting poodles of a few seconds before. They were quite solid—just as real as you and I. For every person on the planet there was now also a poodle, which naturally caused a lot of confusion—both for the humans *and* the poodles!

Mr and Mrs McHaversack, an elderly couple from Dumfries in Scotland, had gone to bed early because they'd had a long day in the countryside, hunting for wild haggis by tossing cabers at them. They were so tired that they slept through the thunderclap and all the rumbling. Mr McHaversack had made a few rumbling sounds of his own, but they had more to do with the baked bean sandwiches he'd had before going to bed than with the fabric of the universe being completely altered. But the loud sound of air rushing to fill a vacuum woke Mrs McHaversack.

'Mc-yawn,' she went in a thick Scottish accent, wriggling discontentedly under the sheets and refusing to open her eyes. She rolled over slightly to hold on to her husband for comfort, and got the surprise of her life when she felt long curly fur instead of her husband's chin and shoulders.

'Tavish?' she said, her eyes still closed. 'Have ye nae shaved the last few mc-days?'

Then she got the second surprise of her life when she felt a hairy hand reach for *her* shoulders.

'Tavish, hoo could ye?' said the owner of the hand. Her voice was remarkably similar to that of Mrs

McHaversack. 'Ye've shaved off all yeer prize fur, ye beastie!'

Both of them opened their eyes then, and both of them got the third and most startling surprise of their lives. Instead of looking across at her husband, Mrs McHaversack was looking at the poodle version of herself staring wide-eyed back at her. And the poodle was equally as alarmed because she expected to see her poodle husband there.

'Hoots!' screamed the human Mrs McHaversack.

'Mc-woof!' screamed the poodle Mrs McHaversack. And they both leaped out of bed in their tartan pyjamas, running down the stairs and trying to get away from each other. But because they were the same person they did roughly the same things, and they would never get away from each other.

The two Tavishes on the other side of the bed continued sleeping happily. One of them dreamed about winning at the Highland Games; the other dreamed about winning at Crufts.

It was chaos in the Sydney Opera House in Australia. The performance was supposed to be Prokofiev's *Romeo and Juliet*, based on Shakespeare's famous love story, but the atmosphere in there was far from loving. There were now twice as many musicians in the local symphony orchestra—half of them poodles, of course—but still the same amount of instruments. And there was fighting all over the stage as irate musicians battled with their poodle or human equivalents over who should have possession of each instrument. The human clarinetist broke his clarinet over his poodle self's head, knocking him unconscious. That meant he had won, but now he didn't have an instrument to play with, which rather defeated the object of the fight.

Over in the percussion section, one poor poodle had been shoved inside a kettle drum, his legs sticking out of it and waving madly about in all directions. The violinists were shooting their bows at each other, just like a game of cowboys and Indians. And you should have heard the din that was coming from inside the grand piano!

The only person in the orchestra who wasn't fighting was the conductor—the *two* conductors, that is. The human and the poodle conductor stood side by side in front of the stage, continuing to wave their batons in the air as if they were helping to bring to pass a well-choreographed fight scene.

Most of the Australian audience didn't notice all this. They were too shocked at seeing their other selves squeezing tightly next to them on their seats. A lot of them expressed their shock by shouting 'Bruce!' or 'Gidday!' (they didn't know what else to say), and some of the quieter members of the audience nervously twiddled with the corks dangling from strings round the brims of their hats.

The only people who noticed the disappointing lack of music were the Rolf Harris lookalike society sitting near the back. They trundled en masse to the ticket office to demand their money back, some of them trundling with artificial third legs in remembrance of one of Rolf's greatest songs ('Jake the Peg', in case you're not familiar with the wonderful Rolf Harris repertoire). Others were clutching didgeridoos or their precious Rolf Harris wobble boards.

The man and the poodle at the ticket office very kindly agreed to give out refunds, but there was just one problem: should they give the money back to the human members of the society or the poodles?

Until a few minutes ago a very important meeting had been taking place in the main conference room of the United Nations in New York. Diplomats from all over the world had been discussing the issue of global nuclear disarmament, and a lot of progress had been made. There had been one representative from every major country in the world, but now there were two (the extra representatives were poodles, of course), and that was the reason the meeting had temporarily stopped.

'It's a communist plot!' fumed the human American diplomat. 'Those filthy Russian scum planted all these poodles here to halt the disarmament talks.' The *poodle* American fumed this as well.

'Niet, comrade, not true!' retorted the two Russian diplomats in an extremely bad Russian accent because I'm not very good at writing for Russians. 'Diss plot was perpetrated by you American capitalist pig-dogs!' The poodle Russian diplomat said 'pig-humans'.

Other diplomats were in uproar as well, each of them blaming rival nations for the unwanted disruption of the meeting. These accusations turned into fist fights, and the conference room was soon full of poodles fighting fellow poodles and humans fighting humans. It didn't give you much hope for the future of the world when a meeting like this for peace— attended by some of the world's most influential politicians—so easily degenerated into a violent free-for-all with fists and broken bits of furniture flying everywhere.

Scenes like this were happening all over the world.

In a McDonald's in Paris, a poodle, with his human counterpart standing next to him, requested:

'Erm, two McChumburgers with fries, s'il vous plaît, and a box of Kitten McNuggets.'

'Merci, monsieur,' said the poodle assistant behind the counter, but the human assistant poured a cold strawberry milk shake all over her because *she* wanted to serve the customer.

The American space shuttle in orbit above the earth had five new inhabitants.

'Mission control, come in please!' the frightened space shuttle captain screamed into his microphone. 'We've been invaded by horrifying aliens, and they look just like poodles! Please help; we're in terrible danger!'

The poodle version of the captain was also screaming into the microphone: 'Mission control, you've got to help us! We've been invaded by dangerous aliens that look just like horrible human beings! I don't think we're going to come out of this alive!'

At the British Telecom tower in London, the man who read the speaking clock all day long was not keeping up with the times. Like a true professional he was continuing to read the time from a script in front of him, but he was many minutes behind because of an unexpected distraction. You see, he kept glancing nervously at the off-putting poodle who had somehow materialised next to him and who was also trying to read the time—and this was slowing him down considerably. (*You* try talking sensibly when someone keeps saying the same things as you.)

Also, the woman who went 'Beep...beep... beeeeeep!' every ten seconds kept beeping in the wrong places because she felt uneasy about the strange upright poodle standing next to her.

In a quiet street in Walbridge, Penny Green

prodded the poodle in front of her to make sure it was real. The poodle did likewise.

'It's you; it's really you,' said Penny, unusually excited. 'It's my true body. And inside you must be the human "me" that belongs in here.' She patted her human body to show what she was referring to.

'You're right,' said the poodle. 'It's great to see you...I mean, me, again. But now that we've finally met up, just what are we going to do?'

'I don't know.' Penny shrugged her shoulders. 'All I know is that Dickie wants me to help him at 29 Lottbridge Drive.'

'Me too,' said the poodle. 'Come on, let's have a race. Last one there's a Shredded Wheat.'

It would be a matter of seconds before Charlie, Ethel and Professor Boggles in the cage (plus three new poodles in the cage with them), were totally destroyed by the hate ray passing through them. The ray was now thousands of times stronger than the Clothes Line Snatcher ever intended. No longer were they screaming or writhing around on the floor of the cage; they didn't even have the energy for that. There was nothing they could do to stop the constant, unbearable pain. The situation seemed hopeless.

The Clothes Line Snatcher had given up hope as well; everything had gone horribly wrong. He didn't realise quite how hopeless it all was until he and his poodle self despondently crawled over to the operations console, past all the hypnotised bodies whose eyes were now glowing a deep evil red because they were so full of hatred. Even though they were normally black-and-white, the photocopy's eyes were glowing the reddest.

The two Clothes Line Snatchers shuddered with intense horror when they saw from figures on a computer read-out just what the hate ray was doing. Now that it had sliced clean through into the poodle universe so that both the human universe and the poodle universe were unnaturally one, it was busily slicing through into hundreds of other universes. Soon all the different universes would be spilling into each other, and because space wouldn't be able to cope with the astronomical amounts of suddenly overlapping matter, there would almost certainly be one almighty explosion and...BOOM!...*the end of all creation as we know it.*

There was no stopping the hate ray. The two Clothes Line Snatchers certainly couldn't stop it. All of creation was heading for certain destruction, and before the night was through there would be no more earth, no more solar system, no more galaxies...no more *anything*. Quite depressing, really.

'What have I done?' wailed the remorseful human Snatcher. 'This is terrible.' What an understatement! 'All I wanted was unlimited power; is that too much to ask? I had it all figured out. But that Dickie Dustbin kid had to mess things up, didn't he? And now we're doomed. We're all going to die!'

The poodle Snatcher didn't say anything; instead he howled at the top of his voice—a bloodcurdling howl that could be heard for miles around. He was mourning the end of everything. And it was all happening because the Clothes Line Snatcher had stupidly hooked up the wrong sort of person to his hate ray circuit, not realising just how much potential for hatred there was inside him. One small slip-up and, 'Goodbye creation.' What a meaningless way to go.

The pain. The two Charlies in the cage tried to think through all the pain. It was hard, but they must concentrate while they were still able.

'An answer; there must be an answer; there's always an answer.'

Both Charlies refused to believe that this was it for them and their colleagues. But what could they do? They had no strength to help themselves, and neither did anyone else in the cage. It didn't look as if anyone down in the Snatcher's house was going to help them, and everyone else was too wrapped up in their own strange circumstances to come to their aid. So who could the Charlies turn to?

There *was* an answer, and like a flash of inspiration it came to them.

'The man in the white robe. And the being I felt in my bedroom that morning last year, who's looking after the world and probably even the universe. If they're one and the same person, and if he really does love everyone and *is* in control of everything, then maybe *he* can help.'

It was difficult to think straight because of the pain, but the Charlies still managed to reflect bitterly on the effects of the hate ray: 'Destructive power—that's all the hate ray contains. Ultimately, all hatred can do is destroy. It takes a special kind of power to rebuild or create something from scratch. I wonder if the man in the white robe has that power?'

The human and poodle Charlies both felt a new wave of love surge through them that showed them they were thinking along the right tracks. With this new energy inside them, and a confidence that they were right, they slowly lifted their heads and looked straight up into the night sky—which is where they thought they were supposed to look. Then they called out: 'God—or whoever you are—if you're really there, please help us, okay? Otherwise we're done for!'

The Charlies' plea, without them realising, also applied to the situation of the dying universe—with its dying humanity—heading irreversibly for destruction unless someone much bigger than the universe stepped in to make things right.

The human and poodle Pennys stopped breathlessly by the police car outside the Clothes Line Snatcher's house.

'Look at that—puff—beam,' wheezed the poodle Penny, pointing upwards. 'What do you think it's—phew—there for?'

'Never mind the—wheeze—beam,' gasped the human Penny. 'Look who's in the back of the car.'

The poodle Penny peered inside. 'Why, it's Jonathan!' she exclaimed. 'And there's—puff—a human sitting next to him. Is that—gasp—Jonathan as well?'

'Yes,' answered the human Penny, 'but for some reason he's—gulp—not moving, even though his eyes are open. It looks as if he's—pant—in a trance or something, just like the two—puff—policemen by the steering wheel and the other—gasp—police-men on the pavement.'

The two Penny's looked at the poor hypnotised policemen on the pavement, one of them human and one of them a poodle. Then, to their amazement, another policeman appeared, this one a larger-than-normal snail. Then a fourth policeman in the form of a kangaroo. Then an elephant. Then a strange green creature with lots of hair; a three-headed donkey; a blue blobbish-thing wearing sunglasses; a large dragonfly puffing a cigar; and so on and so on until there were hundreds of different policemen crowding the street, all of them the same person in his different forms from all the universes.

And not just hundreds of policemen. There were hundreds of Penny Greens, hundreds of Jonathans, and hundreds of everyone all over the world. The hate ray had broken through into all the universes. Space couldn't take the strain any more; everything started rumbling and shaking and horribly fading in and out, and then, just before the imminent explosion, a giant hand reached down from heaven. Was it in answer to the Charlies' prayer?

All time suddenly stood still.

21

There was darkness.

22

There was still darkness.

23

It was dark for an awfully long time.

24

Gradually, all the different creatures from every single universe regained their consciousness. They felt like they had been asleep for years, which in a way was true because they were now outside time and space where, before you can even say 'Corn Flakes', hundreds of centuries can pass.

What were they seeing while outside time and space? Well, not a lot. You see, their senses weren't equipped to cope with what was presently going on around them—much too mind-blowing. Instead, all the creatures saw deep inside themselves from this unique perspective of being outside all that they'd ever experienced or thought was real.

Some of the creatures saw only relatively insignificant things because that was all they needed to see in this specific stage of their lives. Professor Boggles saw that he needed to buy more than his usual amount of groceries because he had a fellow loony professor from America coming to stay with him next week. Ethel saw how successful her upcoming presentation of Handel's *Messiah* using milk bottles would be, and how much enjoyment it would bring to those in the old people's home.

Some saw that they needed to do something before they could develop as human beings. 'Crusher' Craig saw that he somehow had to make friends with or at least stop hating his father, otherwise he would always be mixed-up and miserable. Mr Hobbs saw that he should be thankful, and not bitter, about all the things he'd done as a single person that he wouldn't have been able to do if he was married. And the Clothes Line Snatcher saw that he needed to do precisely what Charlie Digestives had told him back in his living room in Walbridge: forgive all those he had blamed for the destruction of his beloved Dougall doll all those years ago.

Penny Green was surprised with what she saw: a pleasant scene of her and Jonathan Matthews walking by the river in Walbridge in summertime, holding hands and deeply in love with each other. Jonathan saw exactly the same. It was obvious from this that, at least for the time being, they were meant to be together as boyfriend and girlfriend. They hadn't realised it before, but they must have gradually fallen in love over the last few months of being so close together.

Dickie Dustbin was initially horrified—and also intensely jealous—when he saw this same scene of Penny and Jonathan by the river. But then he saw that he had a bit of growing up and a lot of living to do before he would be granted his female partner. It was a hard truth to swallow, but something that he definitely needed to know. And he smiled when he realised that if he did what he was supposed to with his life, he would meet the right girl for him at just the right time and she would be right for him in every way. Something definitely worth looking forward to.

What Charlie Digestives saw was much more complex and crucial. He was at just the right stage in his life to make a life-changing decision that would affect in every way where he stood in relation to the universe, *and* to the person behind the universe.

He saw himself standing in the dock of a typical British courtroom. The judge at this trial was the photocopy of Dickie Dustbin, dressed in all the typical judge gear and wearing one of those ridiculous grey wigs that judges normally have on their heads. It had lots of white powder in it so that every time the photocopy jerked his head powder flew out in all directions.

The jury was made up of friends and colleagues of Charlie's: Professor Boggles; Jonathan and Penny; the real Dickie Dustbin; Ethel, of course; Sam Spam, his cockney gardener; Rod Winkles, president of the local Bob Monkhouse fan club; and colleagues of his from the ACME Peace Corporation in London, including X, Charlie's boss, an elderly but dominating person, with a gruff voice and constantly stern expression. If he wasn't the head of the ACME Peace Corporation he would have made a very good colonel in the army.

Also in the jury was the man in the white robe, sitting expressionless at the front of the jury box. There was no one else in the courtroom.

The photocopy pounded his gavel up and down a few times because that is what judges are supposed to do. Then he pointed it at Charlie, looking very mean indeed. Charlie wasn't looking forward to what he was going to say.

'Charlie Digestives,' the photocopy started, 'you

have been brought before the court today for the hideous crime of living. You don't deserve to live, Charlie. Your heart is wicked—desperately wicked. Yes, you do try to do good; you have selflessly devoted your whole life to ridding the world of crime. But no matter how many good deeds you perform, no matter how hard you try to be good, you cannot escape the deep darkness that makes up your very being. You deserve nothing but death, Charlie, yet you stubbornly persist in living.'

The photocopy was relishing every word of his accusation, and his eyes screwed up tightly every time he emphasised a particularly important word.

Charlie knew that none of this was really happening—that he was in some sort of bizarre dream. And yet the tension he felt was very real, and he couldn't help sweating. He also couldn't speak because he was so scared. There was something about that creepy judge that made him feel utterly small and helpless. He also felt utterly guilty. It was worse than all the nightmares he'd ever had.

The photocopy turned to the jury, and asked them: 'Jury, have you come to a decision yet about the accused?'

'We have,' they answered in unison.

'Well, then?'

The man in the white robe stood up. He was obviously the head of the jury. He glanced briefly at Charlie, then faced the judge. His face was still expressionless.

'Good,' thought Charlie, 'it's that man again. He's bound to be on my side, isn't he? And with all my best friends in the jury, I shouldn't really come to any harm.'

'We find the accused guilty,' the man stated calmly.

'What?' This was the last thing Charlie expected to hear. He looked at those in the jury and appealed to them: 'I've never done anything wrong to you lot. Why have you all turned against me?' Then he looked at the man in the robe and protested: 'And I thought you were my friend.'

'What can I say?' said the man in the robe. 'I can only speak truth, and you are definitely guilty. You don't deserve to live.' He sat back down again. There was nothing more to say.

The photocopy looked pretty pleased with himself, and his eyes screwed up tightly again with intense satisfaction. He pounded his gavel up and down a few more times, then pointed it at Charlie once more.

'Did you hear that, Charlie? Even the jury agree with me. You are guilty of living, and therefore I have no choice but to take your life away from you. I hereby sentence you to...DEATH!'

Upon the word 'death' the courtroom and its inhabitants completely disappeared. Charlie was now in the middle of a seemingly endless desert, with the blazing sun above beating down hard on him. If he could he would have crawled miles for just a few drops of cool, refreshing water, but that was not possible. He was trapped in some wooden stocks, his hands and feet firmly clamped inside so that he couldn't escape no matter how hard he struggled.

'Help!' he cried. 'Help me, someone, please!' But the situation seemed hopeless, and the shouting only made him thirstier. All he could do now was just wait to die. He didn't know what hurt him more: the

189

fact that he was boiling out here in the sun and thirstier than he'd ever been before, or that it was his so-called friends who had convicted him and caused this punishment.

An hour or so later, just when Charlie thought he could stand the unbearable heat and thirst no more, the man in the white robe could be seen walking over a dune in the distance and heading towards him.

'Go away!' Charlie shouted to him, bitterly. 'I never want to see you again. It's because of you that this is all happening.'

'But you called for help,' the man shouted back, 'and I set off as soon as I heard you.'

'I didn't call for *your* help,' protested Charlie.

'Nevertheless, help is what you're going to get.' The man had reached Charlie now, and he stood in front of him in the stocks. 'Now, *do* you want me to help you, or *don't* you?'

'I...'

'This is important now, Charlie. I won't help you unless you ask me to.'

It didn't take long for Charlie to make up his mind. He was in a desperate situation, and he would be foolish to turn down any offer of help, no matter who it was from.

'Yes, yes, you help me, please. I can't take this terrible heat any longer.'

The man in the white robe smiled. It was such a loving smile that Charlie was taken aback by it. Was this really the same man who had proclaimed him guilty from the jury box?

The man knelt down on the hot sand and, with just the right key that he happened to have in his pocket, he proceeded to release Charlie from the wooden stocks. Charlie was too weak to do anything but limply slide out of them.

'Thank you,' he said, panting on the ground, exhausted by this sudden exertion.

The man in the white robe didn't say anything. Instead, he sat down where Charlie had been and put his own hands and feet in the stocks.

'Lock me up, Charlie,' he demanded, glancing down at the key next to him on the ground.

'What?'

'I said, lock me up. Your life deserves death, Charlie. Someone's got to die. If I do it, you can go free.'

The man in the robe was still smiling. Charlie was so choked up by this extraordinary kindness that he could barely speak. He just about managed to say: 'I…I don't deserve this.'

'I know you don't,' said the man. 'Come on, Charlie, lock me up, quickly. You have your whole life ahead of you now and I don't want you to waste a second of it.'

Charlie did as he was told. Part of him didn't want to, but he knew that his life depended on it, and the man was so insistent that Charlie obeyed. He felt so awful as he turned the key in the lock because he was condemning an innocent man to death. Why was this man, whom he barely knew and whom he'd never done any great favours, so willing to die in his place? It was because he loved him, that was why, but Charlie found that hard to grasp because he didn't believe such a superhuman love was possible, especially when it was directed towards him.

As soon as the difficult deed was done, Charlie stood up again and threw the key back down on the ground.

191

'Bye, Charlie,' said the man, now smiling a weary sort of smile. 'Your criminal record has been wiped clean. I am taking your punishment for you. Go. Enjoy your new life. And don't forget me, Charlie, will you?'

'No—never,' insisted Charlie, then the man died before his eyes before he had a chance to realise what was going on. It only took seconds. As soon as he'd said his last words to Charlie, he mumbled a few words to the sky, closed his eyes and gently collapsed at the stocks. No heartbeat any more. No pulse. He was dead.

The scene changed once more. Charlie was floating in a cool, blue ocean that stretched out to the horizon in all directions.

At first he didn't notice the change. He was too stunned by the sacrifice of the man in the white robe. He didn't cry over the man's death; he was just puzzled as to why anyone would do such a thing for him.

Then he looked down and around. Gone was the searing, unbearable heat of the desert; now he was in all this wonderful cool water. He tasted some. There was no salt in it—perfect drinking water. So refreshing.

And he was free. Free to swim in these waters for as long as he wanted. He was alive and free. Totally free.

'Yippee!' he screamed, excitement pulsing through every vein in his body. This was the happiest moment of his life.

He swam for miles, laughing and screaming all the way. He'd never expressed himself like this before, normally keeping his emotions to himself. But something wonderful had happened: his life had been given back to him and he wanted everyone to know!

For hours he swam. But the time came when he could swim no more. He had run out of energy and he desperately gasped for air while flapping his arms up and down in the water to keep himself afloat.

There was a 'splish splosh' sound behind him, and soon, standing on the water in front of him, was the man in the white robe. He wasn't weary now; he looked full of strength. And he smiled down at Charlie.

Charlie was confused. 'Puff—I thought—phew—you were dead,' he said between gulps.

'I was,' said the man. Then he changed the subject. 'You forgot me, didn't you? I told you not to. Now look what's happened. Come on, you silly thing; take my hand.'

Charlie obeyed, and the man lifted him up so that he was also standing on the surface of the water. Charlie was amazed; he didn't think such a thing was possible.

The man let go of Charlie's hand and started to walk away, treading lightly over the gentle waves. 'Come,' he said, 'follow me.'

'But...' Charlie hesitated for a few seconds, but as soon as he felt his feet sliding back into the water, he quickly put one foot in front of the other, then again, then again, until he was somehow walking on the water's surface. He wasn't very confident about it (would *you* be?), but with some practice he would soon be a lot more skilled.

'That's it, Charlie,' encouraged the man in the robe, glancing behind him while he continued to walk away. 'This is all I want from you in your new life. A lot easier, isn't it? Not like all that silly thrashing about in the water. That just leads to exhaustion. From now on, will you do things my way, Charlie, and at my speed? And will you go wherever I go?'

'Yes, yes of course I will,' said Charlie. He had done a lot of different things in his eventful life, but only now did he feel he was fulfilling the task he was born to. 'I will follow you anywhere,' he promised. And he meant it.

The man in the robe urged Charlie forward with a wave of his finger, and Charlie reverently followed him towards the distant setting sun.

Charlie didn't intend to stop until he'd reached it.

25

Everyone awoke from their dreams, or visions, or whatever you want to call them. Everyone was back in the universe where they belonged, and they somehow knew that things had gone back to the way they should be. All were pretty much shell-shocked. They didn't realise it, but in their own different ways they had all had an encounter with infinity, *and* with the Infinite. Cor!

In the human being universe (and in all the other universes) there were an awful lot of people crammed together in the Clothes Line Snatcher's living room: the Clothes Line Snatcher, the thirty people he'd hypnotised at his party (they were no longer connected up to each other), Charlie, Ethel,

Professor Boggles, Jonathan Matthews, Penny Green, the two Dickie Dustbins, and those two policemen from Parts Two and Three. In short, all of the stars of this wonderful book were there...except for one.

All in the room seemed lost, and as they looked across at each other their expressions said: 'So what happens next?'

What happened next was the man in the white robe materialising in front of the now inactive hate ray amplifier, almost like the Enterprise crew does in *Star Trek*, except he wasn't bathed in shimmering, sparkling lights and his coming wasn't accompanied by unearthly sound effects. As soon as he had fully materialised, there was a piercing, blood-curdling scream from the photocopy of Dickie Dustbin, and he disintegrated into a pathetic pile of ashes on the floor. The man in the robe radiated pure goodness wherever he went, and the photocopy, who merely radiated evil, was destroyed when he appeared.

Everyone in the room faced the man in the robe. They instinctively knew that he had something to do with all the universes being put back where they belonged, and with the visions they'd seen. In this universe they were seeing him as a human being, but in other universes they saw him as one of their own. You see, it wasn't his appearance that mattered, but who he represented.

They quietly waited for him to speak, obviously expecting some sort of profound statement. But for a number of seconds he didn't say anything. He just surveyed the whole living room, giving everyone the sort of stern look that a disappointed father would give to his favourite child who'd just misbehaved.

When he did say something, it was just four words: 'Don't do it again.' And he uttered them to everyone—not just the Clothes Line Snatcher—as if they were all in some way partly responsible for the near-destruction of the universe.

Everyone was ashamed. All felt guilty in his presence, and rightly so. It was hard to look straight into his face, so most in the room looked down at the floor, many of them trying to pretend that he wasn't there at all.

The only person who did look at him was Charlie Digestives. Charlie hoped more than anything that the man would indicate in some way that he cared for him, just like he had in the dream by freely giving up his life, and also helping him out of the water. But no, why should he? He had far too many things to do, and the only reason he'd appeared to them all was to tell them off. He certainly had no time to bother with someone like Charlie.

Charlie was so wrong.

As if he knew just what Charlie was thinking, the man turned to him, smiled, and said, 'I know you.'

I know you! Wow! The man who'd saved the universe—someone that important—*knew* someone small and insignificant like Charlie.

I know you! Just the thought of it turned Charlie ice cold with awe. Amazing! But he didn't yet know the man's name.

'Who *are* you?' he asked.

The man replied by lifting up his hands.

'What's that supposed to mean?' thought Charlie, but before he could enquire any further the man started to fade away again. He just had two more words to say to Charlie: 'Follow me.' And then he had gone completely.

'Follow you?' shouted Charlie to the space where

the man had been. 'I want to, but I don't know where you've gone. How am I supposed to follow you?'

Another unexpected reply. In answer to his question, Charlie felt a supernatural love surge right through him, similar to the love he'd felt back in the cage when he called out to the night sky. The love was invigorating, and it gave him new hope for his life. Charlie guessed that this love had something to do with following the man, and he hoped that it would never go away.

The love also made him appreciate his friends a lot more, especially Ethel. Ethel with all her odd quirks and habits. Ethel the eccentric. Over the last few years it had been a sort of love/hate relationship between them—ie he loved to hate her. Actually, it was more like putting up with her. She did her job well, in her own unique way, and had surprisingly been a good support for Charlie in his never-ending task of combating the worldwide problem of crime with the ACME Peace Corporation. And so Charlie had managed to put up with her messy ways, her anti-social hobbies and her chronic singing voice that had turned the deadliest criminals into quivering lumps of jelly as they tearfully pleaded with her to stop.

Now Charlie realised that he would never have been able to make it without her, and he was so full of gratitude that he enthusiastically wrapped his arms around her and planted a big, soggy kiss on her forehead.

'Ooh, sir, you've made me go all wobbly,' said Ethel, quite dazed.

Then Charlie saw again in his mind the man in the robe holding up his hands, and he realised the significance. Each hand had a deep red mark on it, didn't it? It was almost as if something sharp, like nails, had been driven right through them. Nails! There was only one character from history Charlie knew who'd had nails driven through his hands. Someone he'd heard about during school assemblies, at Sunday School when his parents took him to church, on boring programmes on the telly on Sundays, and sometimes on short religious bits on the radio in the mornings. But Charlie had assumed that he wasn't real, or that the events of his life had been greatly exaggerated, like the myths of King Arthur or Robin Hood. But he *was* real! He'd been right there in the room with them. And what's more, he *knew* Charlie!

Charlie understood now the meaning of the dream. The man in the dream had died for him so that he could have a new life. Well, it looked like he had done that for him in real life as well. And he had gone through all that suffering all those years ago because he loved Charlie with a love that was more than human.

Charlie couldn't take this. He sobbed his eyes out like a little kid. He hadn't cried in years.

No one in the room went to comfort him. They were all too busy thinking.

26

It was a miserable Friday morning in Walbridge, England—dull and drizzly, and altogether rather unpleasant for those sorts of people who don't like dull and drizzly mornings. Dickie Dustbin was one of those people so he should have felt miserable himself. But he didn't. He was happy. For the first time in months he felt truly happy.

As he walked to Heathlands Secondary School he thought back over the events of the last few days.

Not much happened in the world on Tuesday, for obvious reasons. It's traumatic enough being confronted with your poodle self from another universe, let alone your snail self, your kangaroo self, and then *all* your selves from all the different universes. But then also to be whisked outside of all creation for what seemed like centuries, and to be confronted with the truth of your inner self.... Well, pretty much everyone on the planet was shattered and had a lot to think about, and so hardly anyone went in to work or school (or did what they normally did) on Tuesday. They were in no fit state to do anything.

On Wednesday things were slightly better. For most people it was business as usual, and the governments of the world resumed operation. The President of the United States went on television to announce that all the hallucinations of poodles had been caused by experimental gases being released illegally into the air by those evil communists in the Soviet Union. The President of the Soviet Union replied by accusing the US Army of invading every town in the USSR while dressed up as poodles, just to confuse the locals. And the Animal Liberation Front claimed all responsibility for the poodle phenomenon, saying that if anyone was cruel to animals ever again they'd better watch out 'cause there was more where that came from.

On Thursday Charlie Digestives appeared on worldwide television to give an official account of what happened on Monday evening, but by then public interest had waned and people didn't really take much notice. Much more interesting in the headlines that day was the news that the Queen had sprained her ankle while being pulled around Buckingham Palace on roller skates by her pet corgis (this was the result of an unusual dare by Prince Charles); K-Tel's *The Best of Eerie Church Organ Music Volume 3* had gone platinum, becoming the best-selling album of eerie church organ music ever; and Marcus Bowels from Chipping Sodbury had broken the world record for eating the most baked beans in one day. He'd got through the phenomenal amount of 226,349 tins of Sainsbury's baked beans, and he'd washed them all down with a bathtub full of red-hot curry. Marcus broke another record in the evening, but I don't think we'll go into that.

Now, on Friday, things were pretty much back to normal. It was almost as if Monday evening had never happened. Things hadn't really changed that much. But Dickie Dustbin had changed...for the better.

It wasn't the appearance of the man in the white robe that had done it, although Dickie did feel strangely comfortable (guilty yet accepted at the same time) in his presence. Dickie hadn't a clue who the man was, but he did know that he wouldn't mind seeing him again sometime.

No, it was the dream that had done it; that glimpse into his future. So good to know that if he did what was right, just the right things would happen to him in his life, including eventually meeting the person who would end up as his wife. It was also good to know that Penny Green wasn't the right woman for him. It wasn't good to know this at first, of course; it was pretty hard to take. But it was brilliant when he realised that a great burden had been lifted off his shoulders. He no longer had to worry all the time about whether Penny loved him or not, and he didn't have to go out of his way to impress her and try and be the man he thought she wanted him to be. All he had to be now was himself. That was so liberating!

You know, it didn't even bother him when Penny and Jonathan went out on their first official date on Wednesday night. Penny, who liked Dickie a lot and didn't want to upset him, warned him about the date in the school library that day, and apologised if this would hurt him. But Dickie wasn't hurt at all. Instead he smiled, said he was pleased for them both and wished them a good time together. Penny was so pleased by Dickie's reaction that she leaped up from her seat and gave Dickie a massive great hug, kissing him on the cheek. Everyone in the library looked up at this point, many of them cheering and whistling enthusiastically. Dickie took a bow in front of them all, not embarrassed in the slightest. He was just pleased that Penny still considered him a friend. He didn't realise till he got home that he'd been walking round school since then with lipstick all over his right cheek.

The only thing that had changed for the worse since Monday was the dark side of Dickie's personality returning to him after the photocopy was burned up in the presence of the man in the white robe. But even that wasn't drastically bad news. Dickie was aware now that this side of his personality was there (he wasn't before his photocopy double came on the scene), and he was going to do his best from now on to keep it under control.

On the way to school that morning, Dickie saw the same Coca-Cola can he had encountered twice last week. It was shining as usual, and it almost certainly contained that alien from Planet Yumslurp who may just grant him another wish.

Dickie was pleasantly surprised, and he picked it up and examined it.

'Hmm, if he lets me have another wish, what should I ask for?'

A number of interesting possibilities passed through his mind, but then he thought: 'No, I don't need to wish for *anything*. I'm happy just the way I am.' He defiantly dropped the can onto his foot as he kicked upwards, and the can shot a long way away, eventually landing with a thump in someone's front garden in the distance. As well as the thump, there was an 'Owch!' from inside the can, but there was no one around to hear it.

Dickie whistled a happy tune from the pop charts as he continued walking to school. One good thing about today was that it was the last day of term. He was looking forward to the holidays.

He was also looking forward to the rest of his life.

27

It would be exactly three minutes until Ethel flew through into Professor Boggles' dining room. She was presently skateboarding through the streets of Walbridge with her usual crash helmet and cricket pads on, delivering Charlie's packed lunch to Professor Boggles' house. She had forgotten to give it to Charlie when he left earlier this morning, and he wouldn't be very happy if he didn't get his daily dose of yoghurt and HP Sauce sandwiches.

Charlie Digestives was talking to Professor Boggles in his dining room as he made some important final adjustments to his newly-reconstructed 'Wow' Screen. Charlie was unusually excited and speaking faster than normal, but the professor seemed preoccupied as he poked around with a screwdriver.

'So when I got back home Monday night the first thing I noticed was this big black leather Bible. It had been on my bookshelf for I don't know how many years, but I'd never actually read it before. Now it seemed to be calling to me in my mind, and I knew that it wouldn't stop calling until I'd taken it down off that shelf and read some of it.

'I didn't get any sleep that night, Professor. I spent all night reading about Jesus in the Bible. Have you ever read about Jesus, Professor? He said so many things that made sense, you know; he healed an awful lot of people; and he died for everyone so that whoever wants to live for him can have a new life. Brilliant, eh, Professor? Professor...?'

It would be exactly two minutes until Ethel flew

through into Professor Boggles' dining room.

'Professor, are you listening to me? Have you heard a word I've said?'

Professor Boggles, kneeling next to the screen, reluctantly looked up from his work.

'Giff me a break, please, Charlie,' he requested. 'You'ff been preachink at me all mornink.'

'But this is important,' insisted Charlie. 'Don't you see? He gave me a new life.'

'Yes, yes,' sighed the professor, 'so you keep sayink. But tell me von thing, Charlie; vy iss it dat out off everyvon who voss in der Clothes Line Snatcher's house on Monday, you're der only von who's become a relichious fanatic? And vy, a year ago, vere you der only von to see der man in der vite robe in der Valbridge Museum lecture hall? Vy didn't he show himself to anyvon else?'

'I've been thinking about that, Professor,' admitted Charlie, 'and I reckon that in my case I was so thick-headed that he had to show himself to me personally so that I'd know he was there. I reckon he shows himself to everyone, but not necessarily in such an obvious way. Maybe he shows that he's real through the Bible, through the beauty of nature, through religious television programmes, through music, through people, and maybe through many other ways. I'm convinced that he gives everyone at least one chance—usually more—to choose to live for him. And as for those in the Clothes Line Snatcher's room, I'm praying for them all, even the Clothes Line Snatcher in jail right now. I'm especially praying for you, Professor. I'm praying that you'll choose to live for him as well. You won't regret it.'

Charlie meant it. His life had real meaning now. Before, he'd just been living for himself, and that

204

meant that ultimately he was heading nowhere. But now he intended to play his small part in God's master plan, and he'd been given a supernatural love inside to help him.

'Thank you for prayink for me, Charlie,' said the professor. 'I'm touched.' But you could tell that he wasn't. As far as he was concerned, the appearance of the man in the white robe in the Clothes Line Snatcher's living room was just a mass hallucination, caused by the shock of everyone suddenly being transported back to the universe where they belonged. He thought that Charlie was taking things a little bit too far. As for what Ethel thought of the man in the robe—well, it never really occurred to her to wonder who he was. Ethel lived in a world of her own, and what a strange world it was!

Speaking of Ethel, it would be exactly one minute until she flew through into Professor Boggles' dining room.

The professor stood up and wiped the dust from his typically messy laboratory coat.

'Finished,' he announced, smiling. 'At last, mein "Vow" Screen iss operational again.'

'Congratulations,' said Charlie. 'Now you can continue your studies on life in other universes.'

'Nein.' The professor looked sad.

'What do you mean?'

'Charlie, diss whole mess vith der Clothes Line Snatcher undt der near-destruction off der universe vouldn't haff happened if it vasn't for mein "Vow" Screen. Diss machine iss too dangerous, especially if it gets into der wrong hands. I've destroyed der blueprints so dat no von can make a replica, and ass soon ass I've had von more look into der screen I'm goink to dismantle der whole thing for good.'

'Are you sure, Professor?'

'Perfectly sure.' He turned the 'Wow' Screen on, and could soon see his dining room in the poodle universe, with his poodle self and the poodle Charlie Digestives staring back at him.

'Cor,' said Charlie, and the poodle Charlie on the screen could be seen saying it as well. The picture wasn't as clear as it had been a year ago because the professor had used a few different components this time—but the principle was basically the same.

'Now, if you'll excuse me for a vile,' said the professor, 'I just need to get some extra groceries for mein loony professor friend who's stayink vith me next veek. If you vont to haff a kvick look, I von't turn der screen off till I get back.'

'Okay.' Charlie didn't mind the professor leaving him. He was fascinated by the image on the screen, the first time he'd seen into another universe. He waved to his poodle equivalent on the screen who waved back at exactly the same time.

Ethel was merrily skateboarding up Professor Boggles' garden path, intending to stop as soon as she reached the front door. But the front door opened, and she stupidly saluted the professor in front of her—stupidly because this didn't give her time to stop. The skateboard crashed into the front step, and she flew off it and over the professor, knocking him backwards in his hallway.

'Gesundheit!' he yelled.

Ethel flew right on into Professor Boggles' dining room and bashed into the back of Charlie who was gazing into the 'Wow' Screen.

'Aaaah!' screamed Charlie as he helplessly plunged headfirst into the screen, disappearing inside. His disappearance was immediately followed

206

by an almighty explosion with sparks and bits of the 'Wow' Screen flying everywhere, and smoke rising from the remains of the screen. A few split seconds later there was an unearthly sucking sound as the screen mysteriously reconstructed itself and all the sparks and smoke were sucked back inside. Charlie was then belched back out of it before it finally collapsed on the dining room floor in a thousand-or-so pieces, screws and bolts rolling away from it and the screen itself completely ripped to shreds because of Charlie jumping in and out of it.

'Duh,' went Charlie on the floor. He was so dazed that whistling birds were flying in a circle above his head.

Ethel, covered in ashes and her hair standing on end because of the explosion, handed Charlie what was left of his smoking packed lunch box.

'Here you are, sir,' she said, kneeling in front of him. 'It's your favourite. Yoghurt and HP...oo-er! You've changed!'

Professor Boggles appeared at the doorway of the dining room.

'Mein goodness!' he exclaimed. 'Diss iss terrible!' He wasn't referring to the second destruction of his 'Wow' Screen; that was going to be dismantled anyway. He was referring to the present state of Charlie.

You guessed: it wasn't the human Charlie Digestives who was belched back out of the 'Wow' Screen; it was the poodle Charlie, and that was who was now lying on the dining room floor. And he was fully poodle—not the human Charlie in a poodle body. This different result had happened because of the slight difference in the construction of the screen.

'It'll take me years to get him back vere he belongs,' the professor admitted sadly. 'I destroyed der blueprints off der "Vow" Screen and I can't remember how to put it back together.'

'Crumbs,' said Ethel.

Charlie didn't say anything. He had a phenomenal headache, and he just wanted to crawl away somewhere and die.

Luckily, he didn't. He quickly recovered, and he went on to have lots of exciting adventures as he continued to work for the ACME Peace Corporation in his current canine form.

I'm looking forward to telling you all the adventures of Charlie the Dog, the world's only religious poodle detective. They're brilliant, believe me.

But in the meantime, please buy lots of copies of this book. *Oodles of Poodles* can be used as toilet paper, is just the right size for putting under the short leg of that wobbly table in your kitchen, and you can make great paper aeroplanes out of the pages.

I'll see you all again soon, all right?

There now follows
an exciting preview of
the next stunning
adventure in the
Charlie the Dog series...

Charlie the Dog in...

The Great Baked Bean Scheme

Prologue

It took all the strength she had to drag herself over to the dusty computer screen. She was weary. She had seen much the last few days. Too much.

She had travelled thousands of light years, on the run from the universe's most feared intergalactic space pirates who were after her life...and more. They had chased her through the violent meteor storm in the Antilles sector of the Milky Way galaxy, they had skirted round the Magellan system just before its sun went supernova; they had strayed perilously close to the infamous Rigel hole, very nearly being sucked inside to what would have been eternal death—in a state of not-quite-alive, not-quite-dead, for the rest of time—and now they'd followed her to Loch Ness in Scotland on planet earth.

It didn't take her long to get to the secret operations room of the Death Ride under the loch. She had passed through its creepy underground tunnels and explored its dark mysterious caves many times before, and she knew its maze-like layout as well as the back of her hand. But she had had no sleep for weeks, and she was fading fast. The pirates would soon catch up with her, and they would get what they wanted and then kill her. And her chase through space would all have been for nothing.

Unless, of course, someone came to her aid. That was why she was sitting at the computer. She was going to contact an old friend of hers, the only person she knew on this planet who'd be able to help her.

She wheezed heavily as she punched out on the keyboard the address of her friend: 62 Rodmill Road, Walbridge, England. Immediately the relevant information flashed up on the screen:

62 Rodmill Road is the home of world-famous detective Charlie Digestives who works for the ACME Peace Corporation in London. Among the famous cases he has solved are: the much-publicised Case of the Person Who Ate Radioactive Pickled Onions and Turned into Something 'Orrible; the terrifying Case of the Vicar Who Cooked Too Many Fish Fingers; and the intriguing Case of the Living Weather Balloons that Invaded Parliament. This resulted in nationwide inflation. Ha ha! Get it? Balloons…inflation. Actually, this last case was just a joke. Sorry.

She groaned. She didn't like computers that tried to be funny, and 'tried' was definitely the word for it. She went on to read the rest of the information.

Charlie has been awarded a special medal for 'bravery above and beyond the call of duty' by the Queen of England; he is recognised by the United Nations in New York as one of the foremost forces for world peace in our time; and he also shook hands with Cliff Richard once at a jumble sale.

Charlie suffered a major setback last week when he disappeared into an alternative universe where the main life form on earth is poodles. And his poodle equivalent there ended up in *this* universe. He will almost certainly never be able to return. But Charlie the Dog, as he now likes to be referred to, has announced that he intends to continue with his crime-solving career, even though he is now a poodle instead of a human being.

'As long as the ACME Peace Corporation keep me well stocked up with dog biscuits,' Charlie chuckled at a London press conference two days ago, 'I intend to keep combating the worldwide problem of crime until the day I die.'

'Ha ha ha,' all the journalists at the press conference chuckled back because they were all big fans of his.

Living with Charlie is his absent-minded maid, Ethel, who is believed to be at least ninety-two years old. As well as taking care of Charlie's household chores, she is well on her way towards fulfilling her ambition of spelling out the entire works of Enid Blyton using letters on the lids of Smartie tubes.

'A poodle now, eh?' She was smiling. 'I suspected he might have changed a bit in the fifteen years since I've seen him, but I didn't think he'd change that much!' She laughed, then spluttered all over the place. The exertion of the laughing was obviously too much for her.

'My head,' she groaned. It was a migraine. She was blacking out. She had better work quickly before her strength was totally gone.

She punched this question into the computer: 'Are there any baked beans in Charlie's kitchen?'

The screen flashed back: 'Yes, some leftover beans in a bowl in the fridge.'

Good, she thought. She entered the instruction: 'Please locate the bowl's exact co-ordinates in space'; and while the computer was finding them, she took a cassette tape from her jacket pocket and slotted it in the recorder hooked up to the computer. The tape contained all the relevant details for a reconstruction of Norman, her robot slave, when she was held captive in the intergalactic pirates' spacecraft.

There was a beep from the computer to alert her to the fact that the co-ordinates were now being displayed on the screen.

Her head was throbbing more than ever and she could barely keep her eyes open. With the little strength she had left, she punched into the computer one final instruction: 'Please beam all the details on my tape to those co-ordinates.' She pushed the 'play' button on the recorder, slumped back in her chair, and within seconds she was unconscious.

Only Charlie could help her now, but would he get there in time? The pirates could take days to find her, the layout of the Death Ride was that complicated; or they may strike lucky and find her in minutes.

The only thing that was certain was that her safety hinged upon what was currently going on inside the bowl of baked beans in the fridge in Charlie's kitchen.

Ethel had bought the beans at Sainsbury's because they were marked down by 5p. She loved a bargain.

But Ethel was going to get more than she bargained for.

Don't be a pudding!
Buy
*The Great
Baked Bean Scheme,*
on sale at
a bookshop near you!

The Great Baked Bean Scheme

by Andrew Wooding

Charlie the amazing poodle detective is brave and fearless. At least, he thought he was.

But when his long-lost friend **Agatha** returns, **Charlie** is on the trail of a dastardly plot to take over the universe using the earth's rich supply of baked beans. Before him lies the triple horror of the Death Ride, where he has to face the ultimate fear. No one has survived before...

Phoenix
Published by Kingsway

The Oswain Tales

by John Houghton

Four exciting stories that follow the adventures of Peter, Sarah and Andrew in the world of King Oswain, the Ice Maiden, and the talking Animals of the Great Forest.

1. Hagbane's Doom
On their first journey, the children encounter the evil witch Hagbane, who seems certain to bring slavery or destruction to the simple Forest folk.

2. Gublak's Greed
When Princess Alena runs away from home, she takes the priceless Star-Pearl with her. Gublak the Goblin wants it . . . and he can be very tempting.

3. Surin's Revenge
There's trouble brewing in the North, as an army prepares for war with Oswain. Find out how a remarkable woman (the Ice Maiden) and a scruffy dog called Tatters play their part in resisting the enemy.

4. Tergan's Lair
The penguins have stolen the South Pole. A dragon is stirring under the ice. How can the children stop the entry into the world of a new and sinister power that threatens all freedom?

These books can be read as separate stories, but are even more gripping if read in the above order.

Phoenix
Published by Kingsway

The Book And The Phoenix

by Cherith Baldry

Times are hard for most of the Six Worlds. Earth is long forgotten, left behind in a past age when technology brought men and women to the stars.

The old tales tell how, generations ago, the colonists brought with them a belief, a faith, a way of life. But that's almost forgotten now, just a dream for old men.

Until now. Young Cradoc will see a vision of the legendary phoenix that will lead him to a Book. It is only when he discovers the power in the Book that he also learns there are many who will want to destroy it—and anyone who attempts to protect it.

Phoenix
Published by Kingsway

Hostage Of The Sea

by Cherith Baldry

They came from over the sea, a nation of warriors intent on spreading their empire. When they descended upon a small kingdom that served the God of peace, the battle was short. And Aurion, the peaceful King's son, was the ideal hostage to secure victory.

Coming to the fearsome land of Tar-Askar, Aurion meets the strong and proud son of the warrior king. A most unlikely friendship develops—a bond of love that will prove a greater threat to the Tar-Askan empire than the weapons of war.

Also by **CHERITH BALDRY** in the *Stories of the Six Worlds: The Book and the Phoenix.*

Published by Kingsway

The Muselings

by Ed Wicke

One day three scruffy children from an orphanage in the country have a surprise. Rachel, Robert and Alice fall *up* a tree into another world!

Why have they been brought into the land that scheming Queen Jess calls her own? The Queen and the children would *both* like to know, and as they try to find out, they stumble into hilarious and hair-raising adventures. Here we meet Lord Lrans, mad on hunting; the Reverend Elias, beloved but misunderstood vicar; Ballbody, a round, bouncy fellow...and the Muselings—kind, furry creatures whose world the children have fallen into.

Then Elias faces Queen Jess on a hilltop, and everything changes.

Phoenix

Published by Kingsway

Screeps

by Ed Wicke

'Up the tunnel was travelling something which twisted and slithered and slapped the walls with its scaly skin. It was several yards long, and its body was as thick as a man's. Its eyes were fixed on them, and its forked tongue flicked in and out as it writhed up the slope...'

They were meant to be on a walking holiday with Elias and Nobby, but somehow it had all gone wrong. So Rachel and Rob had to find the friendly Screeps themselves, braving first the Flitters and now the Kraal.

But why was the Queen of Avalon in the dungeons? How did Alice's ice cream end up in Lrans' pocket? What were these Daroks which the Screeps feared? And what was the answer to the worm king's riddle?

Phoenix

Published by Kingsway

The Will Of Dargan

by Phil Allcock

Trouble has darkened the skies of the Realm: the Golden Sceptre crafted by the hands of Elsinoth the Mighty has been stolen. Courageous twins, Kess and Linnil, team up with an assorted company of elves and crafters—and set out to find it.

Their journey takes them through rugged mountains, gentle valleys and wild woods to the grim stronghold of Dargan the Bitter. Will they win back the Sceptre? The answer depends on their courage, friendship and trust.

Phoenix

Published by Kingsway

In Search Of The Golden Sceptre

by Phil Allcock

The evil Dargan has stolen not only the Golden
Sceptre but also Linnil, who is locked in an
underground cell. Kess and his friends set off across
the Realm once again to search for both Linnil and
the Sceptre.

Through clinging, dangerous mists to the northern
kingdom of the extraordinary Ice People, and the
beautiful but treacherous Jewelled Forest—they
struggle onwards. Only the love of Elsinoth and the
strength of their friendship can sustain them, but will
these be enough to thwart the devious plans of
Dargan?

Phil Allcock is also the author of *The Will of Dargan*, as well
as short stories for BBC TV.

Phoenix
Published by Kingsway

THE PHOENIX
CHRISTIAN
FAMILY
C ★ L ★ U ★ B

If you've enjoyed reading this book, and would like to know more about Phoenix children's books, why not become a member of The Phoenix Family Club? Every two months in *Christian Family* magazine you can read two packed pages of news, reviews, jokes, and interviews about our books — hosted by the lovable Phileas Phoenix — and you'll have a chance to contribute something yourself. And if you become a member of the club, for the same price as most of our paperbacks you will receive a badge, a membership card, yet more regular news from Phileas Phoenix, a Phoenix book — *and* a special Free Token Form, exclusive to members of the club.

Below you will see a Phoenix savings token, which can also be found in other Phoenix paperbacks. Six of these tokens, stuck down on the Free Token Form, will get you another Phoenix paperback absolutely free.

For details on how to join the club, read *Christian Family* magazine, or send a stamped addressed envelope to: Phoenix, 1 St Anne's Road, Eastbourne, East Sussex BN21 3UN, England.

COLLECT SIX GET ONE
FREE
SAVINGS TOKEN
Cash value:
0.01p

Phoenix
Published by Kingsway